ST. DANIEL'S CHURCH
7007 Holcomb Road
Box 171
Clarkston, Michigan 48016

THE SILENT PLAYMATE
A Collection of Doll Stories

Fi
Le

THE
SILENT
PLAYMATE

A COLLECTION OF DOLL STORIES

edited and with an introduction by

NAOMI LEWIS

illustrated by

HAROLD JONES

1948

MACMILLAN PUBLISHING CO., INC.
New York

Illustrations © Harold Jones 1979
Arrangement and original material © Naomi Lewis 1979
All rights reserved. No part of this book may be reproduced
or transmitted in any form or by any means, electronic or
mechanical, including photocopying, recording or by any
information storage and retrieval system, without
permission in writing from the Publisher.
Macmillan Publishing Co., Inc.
866 Third Avenue, New York, N.Y. 10022
First American edition 1981
Printed in the United States of America
10 9 8 7 6 5 4 3 2 1

Library of Congress Cataloging in Publication Data
Main entry under title:
The silent playmate.
Bibliography: p.
Summary: An anthology of doll stories, poems, and
excerpts from novels drawn from a variety of sources.
1. Dolls—Literary collections. 2. Children's literature.
[1. Dolls—Literary collections. 2. Literature—
Collections] I. Lewis, Naomi. II. Jones, Harold, date.
PZ5.S587 1981   [Fic]   80-27477   ISBN 0-02-758590-5

CONTENTS

INTRODUCTION

Of all real toys that we know about, none can ever have had so strange and, indeed, enviable a lot as a box of wooden soldiers given to a boy in 1826. The boy was Branwell Brontë, and the toys helped to kindle a fire of writing in each of the Brontë children that would—for the girls at least—stay alight as long as they lived. Here is how Charlotte, in one of the many "secret" papers written in doll-size writing on tiny pages, described the event. By "plays" she means invented games, daydream stories; later they would be set down at once, not "acted".

. . . All our plays are very strange ones. Their nature I need not write on paper, for I think I shall always remember them. The *Young Men's* play took its rise from some wooden soldiers Branwell had . . . Papa bought Branwell some wooden soldiers at Leeds; when Papa came home it was night and we were in bed, so next morning Branwell came to our door with a box of soldiers. Emily and I jumped out of bed, and I snatched one and exclaimed, "This is the Duke of Wellington! This shall be the Duke!" When I had said this Emily likewise took up one and said it should be hers; when Anne came down, she said one should be hers. Mine was the prettiest of the whole, and the tallest, and the most perfect in every part. Emily's was a grave-looking fellow, and we called him "Gravey". Anne's was a queer little thing, much like herself, and we called him "Waiting-Boy". Branwell chose his, and called him "Buonaparte".

And here is Branwell's own account. How much it tells in the last few lines!

The truth respecting the Young Men is when I first saw them in the morning after they were bought I carried them to Emily, Charlotte and Anne. They each took up a soldier, gave them names, which I consented to, and I gave Charlotte Twemy (Wellington), to Emily Pare (Parry) and to Anne Trott (Ross) to take care of them though they were to be mine and I to have the disposal of them as I would—shortly after this I gave them to them as their own.

Never mind the change of names (Parry and Ross were admired explorers)—the toys had served their purpose.

For the doll and child relationship is not as simple and crude as the non-doll-liker desires to think. Make no mistake—unless this happens to be the play of the moment (I use the word as the Brontës used it)—the child is not the parent of the doll, nor the doll the child of the child. For the very young the doll can be the first really private and personal friend and ally. That piece of old blanket? Blanket, forsooth! A year or two later, the doll might be both playmate and confidant in a problematic world; a child with too many brothers and sisters can be as much in need of a private friend of the doll kind as the "only" child. In this doll-child alliance is a hint, a foreshadowing of those later child-and-child friendships, that begin as suddenly as they end, that seem (as with dolls) so close and perfect while they last, yet leave (as again with dolls) a sense of something finally unexplored, an ultimate unplumbed silence which can never quite be reached. Well, it is right that this should be so, or we would not advance at all.

My own experience seems to tally most with that of the Grahame children in *A Departure*—not for the untimely wrenching away of the toys but for their role in the children's lives. A doll or toy would appear from this or that donor, for this or that child, be gazed at with anxious hope, be given a name, then would start to take its uncomplaining part in the difficult nine-and-under world. My "best" doll, to whom I had given the exotic name of Joan, perished through serving too often as the corpse of Caesar to my older brother's Mark Antony. In this much-acted scene my sister and I were invariably first, second, third and fourth Citizens —roles which have always remained for me potent and meaningful. Other dolls were more durable. Why were they not used?

My younger brother, the real original of the family, favoured toy monkeys, to whom he gave such names as Diggely, Surroundus, Fizzli, Nidro Ammonnia; one though was given the still more mysterious name of Bonamy Dobrée. Their general surname was Taddle. They lived in a land called Cadington. A literary ancestor called Semlin Taddle was their Shakespeare. Plays of his occasionally appeared in little booklets, in the neat hand

ST. DANIEL'S CHURCH
7007 Holcomb Road
Box 171
Clarkston, Michigan 48016

of the seven-year-old amanuensis. One play (after a visit to London) was called "Do You Like Bus or Tube Best?"

Something must be said about what is, and what is not, included in this book. Each item here, prose or verse, fact or fiction, has a completeness in itself, though in a very few cases it is also part of a longer work. But, as it happens, some of the best of all doll-stories—*Poor Cecco, The Mouse and His Child*, for instance, are also full-length novels. And because of their skill in design, they do not cut up well into anthology pieces. Other, very small short stories, such as *Emma's Doll, The Little Girl and the Tiny Doll* and *The Night Ride* (or, indeed, the much longer brisk verse saga, the Uptons' *Two Dolls and a Gollywog*) appear to me inseparably wed to their own pictures. Pooh and his fellows also seem to belong to their own context. But to make clear that these are only seeming omissions, I have added a list of doll-books at the end.

Doll-tales, like animal tales, are of two main kinds: those told doll-view (say, *The Steadfast Tin Soldier*), and those told human-view (say, *Elizabeth*). The first kind has more failures, but also the high successes. I have named two of these: *The Mouse and his Child*, moving, poignant and strange; *Poor Cecco*, bright and sunlit; I would add to these *Miss Hickory* and some of the long doll-tales of Rumer Godden. If only one can take top place, it must, I think, be *Poor Cecco*, because its dolls, for all their range and variety, are truly dolls, through and through. Cecco, a loose-jointed wooden dog, used to being left out in all weathers, is the cleverest and most enterprising of all the toys. With Bulka, a tearful fat rag puppy, always giving at the seams, he sets out on a journey to see the local world. And what a journey! I have read this glorious story many a time, with unfailing pleasure, each time lighting on some new flash of insight or wit. Need I say that both these books, Hoban's and Bianco's, have as much in them for adults as for child readers?

In the second kind, the doll as seen from human view, one book seems to me of particular interest—Mrs Hodgson Burnett's *The Little Princess*. Although it is not included in the present anthology, the story deserves the attention of all doll story readers. Little Sara Crewe, whose father is about to leave for foreign lands, explains that she does not need many dolls— just one. "Dolls ought to be intimate friends. Emily is going to be my intimate friend." And who, she is asked, is Emily? "She is a doll I haven't got yet. . . . She is a doll papa is going to buy for me. We are going out together to find her. . . . She is going to be my friend when papa is gone. I want her to talk to about him."

Emily soon becomes this needed confidant. "We must be very great friends to each other and tell each other things. Emily, look at me. You have the nicest eyes I ever saw—but I wish you could speak." Sara decides that dolls *can* read and talk and walk—but not until humans are out of the room. It is only when her belief in herself begins to waver (this is at a time of direst trouble) that her doll belief wavers too. She makes the curious remark, "Perhaps Emily is more like me than I am like myself."

Memory is an amazing acrobat, but not much of a critical judge. I originally thought to start this book with Mark Lemon's *The*

Enchanted Doll (1846). As a child I possessed a small square copy of this, with the Doyle pictures, printed on shiny pages which clove together in damp. Since it was a very small pocket-size, I kept it in a small pocket, and read it constantly. But reading it again in the British Museum I found it too long to include, too heavy-going and with elements in it that might not appeal today. Still, it is a curio worth mentioning, and even in this century has had several reprints. Mark Lemon (1809-70) was one of the founders of Punch; the book was dedicated to Dickens' two little daughters.

If you wish to read more of the splendid *Memoirs of a London Doll*, the first two chapters of which are included in this collection, I recommend the 1969 reprint for its excellent introduction (by Margery Fisher) on its unlikely author, Richard "Hengist" Horne.

In the list at the end I have not included totally adult tales in which dolls have a significant part. But for adult readers I add here a few that should not be missed. One is of course that superb brief novel *Little Boy Lost* by Marghanita Laski, where a case of identification in a French war orphanage depends on a doll. Then, too, there is D. H. Lawrence's short story *The Rocking Horse Winner*. Another marvellous short story *The Inside Room* (based on a doll's house known in childhood) stays in my mind, but not the author's name, nor the book where I found it. (Help, some-one.) And all who have seen the haunting film of *Citizen Kane* will know why I mention it here.

In life, a time comes when the magic, two-way link between child and doll grows thin, is gone. But is not lost: it moves into other paths. Another name for it is imagination. Dolls, like humans, are mortal; they can perish in many ways. And yet they persistently live, as many of these stories, based on real remembered dolls, will show. Could a cricket bat be thrown away? asks Arthur Waley. Could such a fate have befallen the Brontës' wooden soldiers? It could, and yet it could not. For as long as people read, they will remain as alive as ever they were.

Many people have helped with suggestions and some with actual books—notably Mrs Margery Fisher, Mrs Joan South, Mrs Marguerite Dowdeswell. To these, my lasting thanks. And special gratitude goes to Andrea Debnam, Val Shapiro and Linda Scott of Holborn Library for their tireless and imaginative help.

Most dedications seem to me to exclude the reader; so, I tend to refrain from making them. But in this case I hope that readers will not object if the book is informally dedicated to these loyal and silent playmates Joan and Helen and Nancy and Dicky and Jack Bow-Wow and Bruin and Peter Scott (the Arctic explorer doll) and Pegasus the wooden horse, and others—and, of course, Diggely, Surroundus, Fizzli, Nidro Ammonnia, and Bonamy Dobrée Taddle. Not to mention the sack of wooden bricks.

NAOMI LEWIS

THE SILENT PLAYMATE
A Collection of Doll Stories

THE LOST DOLL

Charles Kingsley

"Don't go away," said all the children; "you haven't sung us one song."

"Well, I have time for only one. So what shall it be?"

"The doll you lost! The doll you lost!" cried all the babies at once.

So the strange fairy sang . . .

The strange fairy, if you don't know, is Mrs Doasyouwouldbedoneby in *The Water Babies*, and the song she sang is the one here, the doll-rhyme that most people seem to remember even if they don't recall who wrote it. Mrs Kingsley's memoirs tell us how at breakfast one fine morning in 1862, Kingsley (then Rector of Eversley in Hampshire) was reminded of a promise. "Rose, Maurice and Mary have got their book and baby must have his." The story of the little sweep was begun that day. "Baby" was Greville Kingsley, to whom the book was dedicated. He did rather better than his older brothers and sisters, for *The Water Babies* (first published in 1863) remains his father's outstanding work for the young.

I once had a sweet little doll, dears,
    The prettiest doll in the world;
Her cheeks were so red and so white, dears,
    And her hair was so charmingly curled.
But I lost my poor little doll, dears,
    As I played in the heath one day;
And I cried for her more than a week, dears;
    But I never could find where she lay.

I found my poor little doll, dears,
    As I played in the heath one day:
Folks say she is terribly changed, dears,
    For her paint is all washed away,
And her arm trodden off by the cows, dears,
    And her hair not the least bit curled:
Yet for old sakes' sake she is still, dears,
    The prettiest doll in the world.

THE MEMOIRS OF A LONDON DOLL

"Why sir," said the boy, *"if you please I want a nice doll for my little sister, and I will give you this large Twelfth-cake that I have in paper here for a good doll."*

"Let me see the cake," said the master . . .

This story here is the opening episode of *The Memoirs of a London Doll* (1846). A superb doll classic, it is not only a captivating story but a vivid document about child-life at different social levels in the earliest years of Queen Victoria's reign. To be sure it is all observed doll-view, but the doll sees much and records exactly. "Children do like and delight in circumstantial detail," noted the author. Why is Richard Henry (or "Hengist") Horne —alias "Mrs Fairstar"—not better known today? Perhaps because he did so many unlikely things in his restless life (1802–84), never waiting to make a fixed reputation in any.

But what concerns us here is the time when he was writing about the London doll. He was already a friend of Dickens, Mayhew, Mark Lemon, the Howitts, Elizabeth Barrett (later Mrs Browning), who all in their writing drew attention to the wretched lives of the working or workless poor. Horne himself had served as government investigator into conditions of child-labour in mills and factories. But because he was writing a book for children's pleasure he never overstressed the hardships of the little dancers and milliners and others, though they are certainly there.

THE MEMOIRS OF A LONDON DOLL

Mrs Fairstar

In a large dusky room at the top of a dusky house in one of the dusky streets of High Holborn, there lived a poor Doll-maker, whose name was Sprat. He was an extremely small man for his age, and not altogether unlike a sprat in the face. He was always dressed in a sort of tight pinafore and trousers, all in one, that fitted close to his body; and this dress was nearly covered with dabs of paint, especially white paint, of which he used most in his work. His family consisted of his wife, and three children—two boys and a girl.

This poor family had but one room, which was at the top of the house. It had no ceiling, but only beams and tiles. It was the workshop by day and the bedroom at night. In the morning, as the children lay in bed, looking up, they could see the light through the chinks in the tiles; and when they went to bed in the evening they could often feel the wind come down, and breathe its cool breath under their nightcaps. Along the wall on one side of the room, farthest from the windows, the beds were laid upon the floor; the largest was for the poor sprat-faced Doll-maker and his wife, the next largest was for the two boys, and the smallest, up in the corner, was for the little girl. There were two windows opposite; and a wooden bench, like a long kitchen dresser, extended from one side of the room to the other, close to these windows. Here all the work was done.

This bench was covered with all manner of things; such as little wooden legs and arms, and wooden heads without hair, and small bodies, and half legs and half arms, which had not yet been fitted together in the joints, and paint pots and painting brushes, and bits of paper and rags of all colours; and there were tools for cutting and polishing, and very small hammers, and several old pill-boxes full of little wooden pegs, and corners of scouring paper, and small wooden boxes and trays full of little glass eyes, and glue pots and bits of wax and bits of leather, and a small red pipkin for melting wax, and another for melting India rubber, and a broken tea cup for varnish, and several tiny round bladders, and tiny tin boxes, all full of things very precious to Mr Sprat in his business.

All the family worked at Doll-making, and were very industrious. Mr Sprat was of course the great manager and doer of most things, and always the finisher, but Mrs Sprat was also clever in her department, which was entirely that of the *eyes*. She either painted the eyes, or else, for the superior class of dolls, fitted in the glass ones. She, moreover, always painted the eyebrows, and was so used to it, that she could make exactly the same sort of arch when it was late in the evening and nearly dark, before candles were lighted. The eldest boy painted hair; or fitted and glued hair on to the heads of the best dolls. The second boy fitted half legs and arms together, by pegs at the joints. The little girl did nothing but paint rosy cheeks and lips, which she always did very nicely, though sometimes she made them rather too red, and looking as if very hot, or blushing extremely.

Now Mr Sprat was very ingenious and clever in his business as a Doll-maker. He was able to make dolls of various kinds, even of wax, or of a sort of composition; and sometimes he did make a few of such materials; but his usual business was to make jointed dolls—dolls who could move their legs and arms in many positions—and these were of course made of wood. Of this latter material I was manufactured.

The first thing I recollect of myself was a kind of a pegging, and pushing, and scraping, and twisting, and tapping down of both sides of me, above and below. These latter operations were the fitting on of my legs and arms. Then, I passed into the hands of the most gentle of all the Sprat family, and felt something delightfully warm laid upon my cheeks and mouth. It was the little girl who was painting me a pair of rosy cheeks and lips; and her face, as she bent over me, was the first object of life that my eyes distinctly saw. The face was a smiling one, and as I looked up at it I tried to smile too, but I felt some hard material over the outside of my face, which my smile did not seem to be able to get through, so I do not think the little girl perceived it.

But the last thing done to me was by Mr Sprat himself, whose funny white face and round eyes I could now see. He turned me about and about in his hands, examining and trying my legs and arms, which he moved backwards and forwards, and up and down, to my great terror, and fixed my limbs in various attitudes. I was so frightened! I thought he would break something off me. However, nothing happened, and when he was satisfied that I was a complete doll in all parts, he hung me up on a line that ran along

the room over head, extending from one wall to the other, and near to the two beams that also extended from wall to wall. I hung upon the line to dry, in company with many other dolls, both boys and girls, but mostly girls. The tops of the beams were also covered with dolls, all of whom, like those on the lines, were waiting there till their paint or varnish had properly dried and hardened. I passed the time in observing what was going on in the room under my line, and also the contents of the room, not forgetting my numerous little companions, who were all smiling and staring, or sleeping, round about me.

Mr Sprat was a Doll-maker only; he never made doll's clothes. He said *that* was not work for an artist like him. So in about a week, when I was properly dry, and the varnish of my complexion thoroughly hardened and like enamel, Mr Sprat took me down—examined me all over for the last time—and then, nodding his head to himself several times, with a face of seriousness and satisfaction, as much as to say, "You are a doll fit in all respects for the most polished society"—he handed me to his wife, who wrapped me up in silver paper, all but the head, and laying me in a basket among nine others papered up in the same way, she carried me off to a large doll-shop not far from the corner of New Turnstile in High Holborn.

I arrived safe at the doll-shop, and Mrs Sprat took me out of the basket with her finger and thumb, keeping all her other fingers spread out, for fear of soiling my silver paper.

"Place all these dolls on the shelf in the back parlour," said the master of the shop. "I have no room yet for them in the window." As I was carried to the shelf I caught a glimpse of the shop-window! What a bright and confused sensation it gave me! Everything seemed so light and merry and numerous! And then, through all this crowd of many shapes and colours, packed and piled and hanging up in the window, I saw the crowds of large walking people passing outside in the world, which was as yet perfectly unknown to me! Oh how I longed to be placed in the shop-window! I felt I should learn things so fast, if I could only see them. But I was placed in a dark box, among a number of other dolls, for a long time, and when I was taken out I was laid upon my back upon a high shelf, with my rosy cheeks and blue eyes turned towards the ceiling.

Yet I cannot say that the time I passed on this shelf was by any means lost or wasted. I thought of all I had seen in Mr Sprat's room, and all I had heard them talk about, which gave me many very strange and serious thoughts about the people who lived in the world only for the purpose, as I supposed, of buying dolls. The conversation of Mr Sprat with his family made me very naturally think this; and in truth I have never since been quite able to fancy but that the principal business of mankind was that of buying and selling dolls and toys. What I heard the master of the shop in Holborn often say, helped to fix this early impression on my mind.

But the means by which I learned very much of other things and other thoughts, was by hearing the master's little girl Emmy read aloud to her elder sister. Emmy read all sorts of pretty books, every word of which I eagerly listened to, and felt so much interested, and so delighted, and so anxious and curious to hear more. She read pretty stories of little boys and girls, and affectionate mammas and aunts, and kind old nurses, and birds in the fields and woods, and flowers in the gardens and hedges; and then such beautiful fairy tales; and also pretty stories in verse; all of which gave me great pleasure, and were indeed my earliest education. There was the lovely book called 'Birds and Flowers', by Mary Howitt; the nice stories about 'Willie', by Mrs Marcett; the delightful little books of Mrs Harriet Myrtle—in which I did *so* like to hear about old Mr Dove, the village carpenter, and little Mary, and the account of May Day, and the Day in the Woods— and besides other books, there was oh! *such* a story-book called 'The Good-natured Bear!' But I never heard any stories about dolls, and what they thought, or what happened to them! This rather disappointed me. Living at a doll-shop, and hearing the daughter of the master of such a wonderful shop reading so often, I naturally expected to have heard more about dolls than any other creatures! However, on the whole, I was very well contented, and should have been perfectly happy if they would only have hung me up in the shop window! What I wanted was to be placed in the bright window, and to look into the astonishing street!

Soon after this, however, by a fortunate accident, I was moved to an upright position with my back against a doll's cradle, so that I could look down into the room below, and see what was going on there.

How long I remained upon the shelf I do not know, but it seemed like years to me, and I learned a great deal.

One afternoon Emmy had been reading to her sister as usual, but this time the story had been about a great Emperor in France, who, once upon a time, had a great many soldiers to play with, and whose name was Napoleon Bonaparte. The master himself listened to this, and as he walked thoughtfully up and down from the back room to the shop in front, he made himself a cock'd hat of brown paper, and put it upon his head, with the corners pointing to each shoulder. Emmy continued to read, and the

master continued thoughtfully walking up and down with his hands behind him, one hand holding the other.

But presently, and when his walk had led him into the front shop, where I could not see him, the shop-bell rang and Emmy ceased reading. A boy had come in, and the following dialogue took place.

"If you please, sir," said the voice of the boy, "do you want a nice Twelfth-cake?"

"Not particularly," answered the master, "but I have no objection to one."

"What will you give for it, sir?" said the boy.

"That is quite another question," answered the master; "go about your business. I am extremely engaged."

"I do not want any money for it, sir," said the boy.

"What do you mean by that, my little captain?" said the master.

"Why, sir," said the boy, "if you please I want a nice doll for my little sister, and I will give you this large Twelfth-cake that I have in paper here for a good doll."

"Let me see the cake," said the master. "So, how did you get this cake?"

"My grandfather is a pastry-cook, sir," answered the boy, "and my sister and I live with him. I went today to take home seven Twelfth-cakes. But the family at one house had all gone away out of the country, and locked up the house, and forgotten to send for the cake; and grandfather told me that I and my sister might have it."

"What is your name?"

"Thomas Plummy, sir; and I live in Bishopsgate street, near the Flower Pot."

"Very well, Thomas Plummy; you may choose any doll you fancy out of that case."

Here some time elapsed; and while the boy was choosing, the master continued his slow walk to and fro from one room to the other, with the brown paper cock'd hat, which he had forgotten to take off, still upon his head. It was so very light that he did not feel it, and did not know it was there. At last the boy declared he did not like any of the dolls in the case, and so went from one case

to another, always refusing those the master offered him; and when he did choose one himself the master said it was too expensive. Presently the master said he had another box full of good dolls in the back room, and in he came, looking so grave in his cock'd hat, and beginning to open a long wooden box. But the boy had followed him to the door, and peeping in suddenly, called out, "There, sir! that one! that is the doll for my cake!" and he pointed his little brown finger up at me.

"Aha!" said the master, "that one is also too expensive; I cannot let you have that."

However, he took me down, and while the boy was looking at me with evident satisfaction, as if his mind was quite made up, the master got a knife and pushed the point of it into the side of the cake, just to see if it was as good inside as it seemed to be on the outside. During all this time he never once recollected that he had got on the brown-paper cock'd hat.

"Now," said the master, taking me out of the boy's hand, and holding me at arm's length, "you must give me the cake and two shillings besides for this doll. This is a young lady of a very superior make, is this doll. Made by one of the first makers. The celebrated Sprat, the only maker, I may say, of these kind of jointed dolls. See! all the joints move—all work in the proper way; up and down, backwards and forwards, any way you please. See what lovely blue eyes; what rosy cheeks and lips; and what a complexion on the neck, face, hands, and arms! The hair is also of the most beautiful kind of delicate light-brown curl that can possibly be found. You never before saw such a doll, nor any of your relations.

It is something, I can tell you, to have such a doll in a family; and if you were to buy her, she would cost you a matter of twelve shillings!"

The boy, without a moment's hesitation, took the cake and held it out flat upon the palm of his hand, balancing it as if to show how heavy it was.

"Sir," said he, "this is a Twelfth-cake, of very superior make. If the young lady who sits reading there was only to taste it, she would say so too. It was made by my grandfather himself, who is known to be one of the first makers in all Bishopsgate street: I may say the very first. There is no better in all the world. You see how heavy it is; what a quantity of plums, currants, butter, sugar, and orange and lemon-peel there is in it, besides brandy and carraway comfits. See what a beautiful frost-work of white sugar there is all over the top and sides! See, too, what characters there are, and made in sugar of all colours! Kings and Queens in their robes, and lions and dogs, and Jem Crow, and Swiss cottages in winter, and railway carriages, and girls with tambourines, and a village steeple with a cow looking in at the porch; and all these standing or walking, or dancing upon white sugar, surrounded with curling twists and true lover's knots in pink and green citron, with damson cheese and black currant paste between. You never saw such a cake before, sir, and I'm sure none of your family ever smelt any cake at all like it. It's quite a nosegay for the Queen Victoria herself; and if you were to buy it at grandfather's shop you would have to pay fifteen shillings and more for it."

"Thomas Plummy!" said the master, looking very earnestly at

the boy; "Thomas Plummy! take the doll, and give me the cake. I only hope it may prove half as good as you say. And it is my opinion that, if you Thomas Plummy, should not happen to be sent to New South Wales to bake brown bread, you may some day or other come to be Lord Mayor of London."

"Thank you, sir," said the boy. "How many Abernethy biscuits will you take for your cock'd hat?"

The master instantly put his hand up to his head, looking so confused and vexed, and the boy ran laughing out of the shop. At the door he was met by his sister, who had been waiting to receive me in her arms: and they both ran home, the little girl hugging me close to her bosom, and the boy laughing so much at the effect of the cock'd hat that he could hardly speak a word all the way.

THE STEADFAST TIN SOLDIER

There—well, the world is full of wonders. He saw that he was in the very room where his adventures had started; there were the same children; there were the same toys; there was the fine paper castle with the graceful little dancer at the door . . . Ah, she was steadfast too.

That little paper dancer—something should be said about her. Andersen had a particular gift for cutting dolls, dancers, flowers, landscapes out of folded paper (open out, and a whole page of dancers appears); you will find such items again and again in his tales. For one sure mark of the Andersen story is the life and personality given to what some might just call *things*—sticks, straw, beetles, egg-shells, and of course toys. *The Steadfast Tin Soldier* is a real piece of human drama—love, loss, courage and loyalty, endurance, deadly peril, wild adventure—and the return. Happy or unhappy ending? You can choose, but I would say definitely, the first.

One thing we should remember is that Andersen's father was a shoemaker by trade (and not a very good one) but by nature a poet, student and man of imagination and ideas. He died when Hans Christian was eleven, but before then had shown the boy how to make toy theatres and how to observe the finest detail in anything down to a blade of grass.

Andersen's own life (1805–75) might have been one of his own fairy tales. Born very poor in a small far northern country, writing in a language that hardly anyone used outside its borders, he became, and remains, one of the best-known writers in the world.

THE STEADFAST TIN SOLDIER

Hans Christian Andersen

THERE were once twenty-five tin soldiers; they were all brothers, for they had all been made from the same tin kitchen spoon. Very smart in their red and blue uniforms, they shouldered arms and looked straight before them.

"Tin soldiers!" Those were the first words they heard in this world, when the lid of their box was taken off. A little boy had shouted this, and clapped his hands; they were a birthday present, and now he set them out on the table. Each soldier was exactly like the next, except for one who had only a single leg; he was the last to be moulded, and there was not quite enough tin left. Yet he stood just as well on his one leg as the others did on their two— and he is this story's hero.

On the table where they were placed there were many other toys, but the one which everyone noticed first was a paper castle; you could see right into the rooms through its little windows. In the front, some tiny trees were arranged round a piece of mirror, just like a lake; swans made of wax seemed to float on its surface, gazing at their reflection.

The whole effect was quite enchanting—but the prettiest thing in the whole scene was a young girl who stood in the castle's open doorway. She too was cut out of paper, but her gauzy skirt was of finest muslin; a narrow blue ribbon crossed her shoulder like a scarf, and was held with a glittering spangle quite the size of her face. This charming little creature held both of her arms stretched out, for she was a dancer; indeed, one of her legs was raised so high that the tin soldier could not see it at all. He believed that she had only one leg like himself.

"Now she would be just the right wife for me," he thought. "But she is so grand. She lives in a castle and I have only a box, and there are twenty-five of us in that! It's certainly no place for her. Still, I can try to make her acquaintance." So he lay down full-length behind a snuff-box which was on the table; from there he had a good view of the little paper dancer, who continued to stand on one leg without losing her balance.

When evening came, all the other tin soldiers were put in their box, and the people of the house went to bed. Now the toys began to have games of their own; they played at visiting, and battles, and going to parties and dances. The tin soldiers rattled in their box, for they wanted to join in, but they couldn't get the lid off. The nutcrackers turned somersaults and the slate pencil squeaked on the slate; there was such a din that the canary woke up and joined in the talk—what's more, he did it in verse. The only two who didn't move from their places were the tin soldier and the little dancer. She continued to stand on the point of her toe; he stood just as steadily on his single leg, and never once did he take his eyes from her.

Now the clock struck twelve. Crack!—the lid flew off the snuff-box, and a little black goblin popped up. There was no snuff inside; it was a toy, a jack-in-the-box.

"Tin soldier!" screeched the goblin. "Keep your eyes to yourself!"

But the tin soldier pretended not to hear.

"All right, just you wait till tomorrow!" warned the goblin.

When morning came, and the children were up again, the little boy put the tin soldier on the window-sill. The goblin may have been responsible, or perhaps a draught was blowing through—anyhow, the window suddenly swung open and out fell the tin soldier, all three storeys to the ground. It was a dreadful fall! His leg pointed upwards, his head was down, and he came to a halt with his bayonet stuck between the paving stones.

The servant girl and the small boy went out at once to look for the tin soldier, but although they were almost treading on him, they didn't see him. If he had called out, "Here I am!" they would have found him easily, but he didn't think it proper behaviour to cry out when in uniform.

It began to rain; the drops fell faster and faster—it was a real drenching storm. When it was over a pair of street-urchins passed. "Look!" said one of them. "There's a tin soldier! Let's put him out to sea."

So they made a boat of newspaper, put the tin soldier aboard, and set the boat in the fast-flowing gutter at the edge of the street. Away it sped, and the two boys ran along beside, clapping their hands. Goodness! What waves there were in that gutter stream, what rolling tides! The paper boat tossed up and down, sometimes whirling round and round, until the soldier felt quite giddy. But he remained as steadfast as ever, not moving a muscle, still looking straight in front of him, still shouldering arms.

All at once the boat entered a tunnel under the pavement. Oh, it was dark, dark as it was in the box at home. "Wherever am I going now?" the tin soldier wondered. "Yes, it must be the goblin's doing. Ah, if only that young lady were sharing this journey with me, I wouldn't care if it were twice as dark!"

Suddenly a large water-rat rushed out from its home in the tunnel. "Have you a passport?" the rat demanded. "No getting through without a passport!"

But the tin soldier said never a word; he only gripped his musket more tightly than ever. The boat rushed onwards and the rat chased after it. Ugh! How it ground its teeth and yelled to the sticks and straws, "Stop him! Stop him! He hasn't paid his toll! He hasn't shown his passport!"

There was no stopping him though, for the stream ran stronger and stronger. The tin soldier could see a bright glimpse of daylight ahead where the end of the tunnel must be, but at the same time he heard a roaring noise which well might have frightened a bolder man. Just imagine! At the end of the tunnel the stream thundered down into a canal. It was as fearful a ride for him as a plunge down a giant waterfall would be for us.

But he was already so near to the edge that he could not stop. The boat raced on, and the poor tin soldier held himself as stiffly as he could. No one could say of him that he even blinked an eye.

All at once the little vessel whirled round three or four times and filled with water to the brim; what could it do but sink! The tin soldier stood in water up to his neck, deeper and deeper sank the boat, softer and softer grew the paper, until at last the water closed over the soldier's head. He thought of the lovely little dancer whom he would never see again, and in his ears rang the words of a song:

Onward, onward, warrior,
Meet thy fate; show no fear.

Then the paper boat collapsed altogether. Out fell the tin soldier—and was at once swallowed up by a fish.

Oh, how dark it was in the fish's stomach! It was even worse than the tunnel, and much more cramped. But the tin soldier's courage was quite unchanged; there he lay, steadfast as ever, his musket still on his shoulder. The fish swam wildly to and fro, twisted and turned, and then became still. Something flashed through like a streak of lightning—then all around was cheerful daylight. A voice cried out, "The tin soldier!"

The fish had been caught, taken to market, sold and carried into the kitchen, where the cook had cut it open with a large knife. Now she picked up the soldier, holding him round his waist between her finger and thumb, and took him into the living room, so that all the family could see and admire the remarkable character who had travelled back in a fish. But the tin soldier was not proud; he thought nothing of it.

They stood him up on the table, and there—well, the world is

full of wonders. He saw that he was in the very same room where his adventures had started; there were the same children; there were the same toys; there was the fine paper castle with the graceful little dancer at the door. She was still poised on one leg, with the other raised high in the air. Ah, she was steadfast too. The tin soldier was deeply moved; he would have liked to weep tin tears, only that would not have been soldierly behaviour. He looked at her and she looked at him, but not a word passed between them.

And then a strange thing happened. One of the small boys

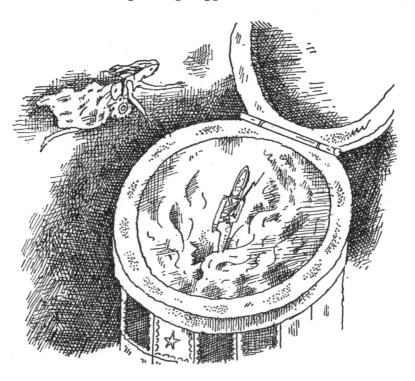

picked up the tin soldier and threw him in the stove. He had no reason for doing this; it must have been the fault of the snuff-box goblin.

The tin soldier stood framed in a blaze of light. The heat was intense, but whether this came from the fire or from his burning love he could not tell. His bright colours were now completely gone, but whether they had faded on the journey or through his sorrow, none could say. He looked at the little dancer, and she looked at him; he felt that he was melting, but he still stood steadfast, shouldering arms. Suddenly the door flew open; a gust of air caught the pretty little paper dancer, and she flew like a sylph right into the stove, straight to the waiting tin soldier; there she flashed into flame and was gone.

Soon the soldier melted down to a lump of tin, and the next day, when the maid raked out the ashes, she found him—in the shape of a little tin heart. What remained of the dancer? Only her spangle, and that was black as soot.

RAG DOLL

Rachel Armstrong
(age 10)

She sat on the floor with her drawers poking out,
Striped socks, black shoes and her hair messed about.
Her dress, black, with flowers,
Her apron white.
If you just left her,
She would stay there all night.

THE DARKEST HOUR IS JUST BEFORE DAWN

Laura watched anxiously while Anna tugged at Charlotte's shoe-button eyes and pulled her wavy yarn hair and even banged her against the floor. But Anna could not really hurt Charlotte and Laura meant to straighten her hair and her skirts when Anna went away.

At last that long visit ended. Mrs Nelson was going and taking Anna. Then a terrible thing happened. Anna would not give up Charlotte . . .

This is a true story; it comes from *On the Shores of Plum Creek*, one of the books by Laura Ingalls Wilder (1865–1959) about her childhood in pioneer Western America a hundred years ago. Laura was no more than six when the great journey began— mother, father and three little girls (later there was a fourth called Grace) travelling by wagon into unknown, unpeopled country. Far, far from shops, towns, or even neighbours the children had few possessions and these they valued much. Why then did parents, even the nicest ones, so often behave like Laura's mother when it came to children's toys? It seems to have been one of the rules of manners, and a bad rule I would say. This story has a happy ending though, as you will see. All the Laura books are worth reading whatever your age. Start with *Little House in the Big Woods* and *Little House on the Prairie*—there are several more. And you won't want to stop or turn back, I promise you.

THE DARKEST HOUR IS JUST BEFORE DAWN

Laura Ingalls Wilder

Now the winds blew cooler and the sun was not so hot at noon. Mornings were chilly, and the grasshoppers hopped feebly until the sunshine warmed them.

One morning a thick frost covered the ground. It coated every twig and chip with a white fuzz and it burned Laura's bare feet. She saw millions of grasshoppers sitting perfectly stiff.

In a few days there was not one grasshopper left anywhere.

Winter was near, and Pa had not come. The wind was sharp.

It did not whiz any more; it shrieked and wailed. The sky was grey and a cold grey rain fell. The rain turned to snow, and still Pa did not come.

Laura had to wear shoes when she went outdoors. They hurt her feet. She did not know why. Those shoes had never hurt her feet before. Mary's shoes hurt Mary's feet, too.

All the wood that Pa had chopped was gone, and Mary and Laura picked up the scattered chips. The cold bit their noses and their fingers while they pried the last chips from the frozen ground. Wrapped in shawls, they went searching under the willows, picking up the little dead branches that made a poor fire.

Then one afternoon Mrs Nelson came visiting. She brought her baby Anna with her.

Mrs Nelson was plump and pretty. Her hair was as golden as Mary's, her eyes were blue, and when she laughed, as she often did, she showed rows of very white teeth. Laura liked Mrs Nelson, but she was not glad to see Anna.

Anna was a little larger than Carrie but she could not understand a word that Laura or Mary said, and they could not understand her. She talked Norwegian. It was no fun to play with her, and in the summertime Mary and Laura ran down to the creek when Mrs Nelson and Anna came. But it was cold. They must stay in the warm house and play with Anna. Ma said so.

"Now girls," Ma said, "go get your dolls and play nicely with Anna."

Laura brought the box of paper dolls that Ma had cut out of wrapping-paper, and they sat down to play on the floor by the open oven door. Anna laughed when she saw the paper dolls. She grabbed into the box, took out a paper lady, and tore her in two.

Laura and Mary were horrified. Carrie stared with round eyes. Ma and Mrs Nelson went on talking and did not see Anna waving the halves of the paper lady and laughing. Laura put the cover on the paper-doll box, but in a little while Anna was tired of the torn paper lady and wanted another. Laura did not know what to do, and neither did Mary.

If Anna did not get what she wanted she bawled. She was little and she was company and they must not make her cry. But if she got the paper dolls she would tear them all up. Then Mary whispered, "Get Charlotte. She can't hurt Charlotte."

Laura scurried up the ladder while Mary kept Anna quiet. Darling Charlotte lay in her box under the eaves, smiling with her red yarn mouth and her shoe-button eyes. Laura lifted her carefully and smoothed her wavy black-yarn hair and her skirts. Charlotte had no feet, and her hands were only stitched on the flat ends of her arms, because she was a rag doll. But Laura loved her dearly.

Charlotte had been Laura's very own since Christmas morning long ago in the Big Woods of Wisconsin.

Laura carried her down the ladder, and Anna shouted for her. Laura put Charlotte carefully in Anna's arms. Anna hugged her tight. But hugging could not hurt Charlotte. Laura watched anxiously while Anna tugged at Charlotte's shoe-button eyes and pulled her wavy yarn hair, and even banged her against the floor.

But Anna could not really hurt Charlotte, and Laura meant to straighten her skirts and her hair when Anna went away.

At last that long visit was ended. Mrs Nelson was going and taking Anna. Then a terrible thing happened. Anna would not give up Charlotte.

Perhaps she thought Charlotte was hers. Maybe she told her mother that Laura had given her Charlotte. Mrs Nelson smiled. Laura tried to take Charlotte, and Anna howled.

"I want my doll!" Laura said. But Anna hung on to Charlotte and kicked and bawled.

"For shame, Laura," Ma said, "Anna's little and she's company. You are too big to play with dolls, anyway. Let Anna have her."

Laura had to mind Ma. She stood at the window and saw Anna skipping down the knoll, swinging Charlotte by one arm.

"For shame, Laura," Ma said again. "A great girl like you, sulking about a rag doll. Stop it, this minute. You don't want that doll, you hardly ever played with it. You must not be so selfish."

Laura quietly climbed the ladder and sat down on her box by the window. She did not cry, but she felt crying inside her because Charlotte was gone. Pa was not there, and Charlotte's box was empty. The wind went howling by the eaves. Everything was empty and cold.

"I'm sorry, Laura," Ma said that night. "I wouldn't have given your doll away if I'd known you care so much. But we must not think only of ourselves. Think how happy you've made Anna."

Next morning Mr Nelson came driving up with a load of Pa's wood that he had cut. He worked all day, chopping wood for Ma, and the woodpile was big again.

"You see how good Mr Nelson is to us," said Ma. "The Nelsons are real good neighbours. Now aren't you glad you gave Anna your doll?"

"No, Ma," said Laura. Her heart was crying all the time for Pa and for Charlotte.

Cold rains fell again, and froze. No more letters came from Pa. Ma thought he must have started to come home. In the night Laura listened to the wind and wondered where Pa was. Often in the mornings the woodpile was full of driven snow, and still Pa did not come. Every Saturday afternoon Laura put on her stockings and shoes, wrapped herself in Ma's big shawl, and went to the Nelsons'.

She knocked and asked if Mr Nelson had got a letter for Ma. She would not go in, she did not want to see Charlotte there. Mrs Nelson said that no letter had come, and Laura thanked her and went home.

One stormy day she caught sight of something in the Nelsons' barnyard. She stood still and looked. It was Charlotte, drowned and frozen in a puddle. Anna had thrown Charlotte away.

Laura could hardly go on to the door. She could hardly speak to Mrs Nelson. Mrs Nelson said the weather was so bad that Mr Nelson had not gone to town, but he would surely go next week. Laura said, "Thank you, ma'am," and turned away.

Sleety rain was beating down on Charlotte. Anna had scalped her. Charlotte's beautiful wavy hair was ripped loose, and her smiling yarn mouth was torn and bleeding red on her cheek. One shoe-button eye was gone. But she was Charlotte.

Laura snatched her up and hid her under the shawl. She ran panting against the angry wind and the sleet, all the way home. Ma started up, frightened, when she saw Laura.

"What is it! What is it? Tell me!" Ma said.

"Mr Nelson didn't go to town," Laura answered. "But oh, Ma—look."

"What on earth?" said Ma.

"It's Charlotte," Laura said. "I—I stole her. I don't care, Ma, I don't care if I did!"

"There, there, don't be so excited," said Ma. "Come here and tell me all about it," and she drew Laura down on her lap in the rocking chair.

They decided that it had not been wrong for Laura to take back Charlotte. It had been a terrible experience for Charlotte, but Laura had rescued her and Ma promised to make her as good as new.

Ma ripped off her torn hair and the bits of her mouth and her remaining eye and her face. They thawed Charlotte and wrung her out, and Ma washed her thoroughly clean and starched and ironed her while Laura chose from the scrap-bag a new, pale pink face for her and new button eyes.

That night when Laura went to bed she laid Charlotte in her box. Charlotte was clean and crisp, her red mouth smiled, her eyes shone black, and she had golden-brown yarn hair braided in two wee braids and tied with blue yarn bows.

Laura went to sleep cuddled against Mary under the patchwork comforters. The wind was howling and sleety rain beat on the roof. It was so cold that Laura and Mary pulled the comforters over their heads.

A terrific crash woke them. They were scared in the dark under the comforters. Then they heard a loud voice downstairs. It said, "I declare! I dropped that armful of wood, didn't I?"

Ma was laughing, "You did that on purpose, Charles, to wake up the girls."

Laura flew screaming out of bed and screaming down the ladder. She jumped into Pa's arms, and so did Mary. Then what a racket of talking, laughing, jumping up and down!

Pa's blue eyes twinkled. His hair stood straight up. He was wearing new, whole boots. He had walked two hundred miles from eastern Minnesota. He had walked from town in the night, in the storm. Now he was here!

"For shame, girls, in your nightgowns!" said Ma. "Go dress yourselves. Breakfast is almost ready."

They dressed faster than ever before. They tumbled down the ladder and hugged Pa, and washed their hands and faces and hugged Pa, and smoothed their hair and hugged him. Jack

waggled in circles and Carrie pounded the table with her spoon and sang, "Pa's come home! Pa's come home!"

At last they were all at the table. Pa said he had been too busy, towards the last, to write. He said, "They kept us humping on that thresher from before dawn till after dark. And when I could start home, I didn't stop to write. I didn't bring any presents, either, but I've got money to buy them."

"The best present you could bring us, Charles, was coming home," Ma told him.

After breakfast Pa went to see the stock. They all went with him and Jack stayed close at his heels. Pa was pleased that Sam and David and Spot looked so well. He said he couldn't have taken better care of everything, himself. Ma told him that Mary and Laura had been a great help to her.

"Gosh!" Pa said. "It's good to be home." Then he asked, "What's the matter with your feet, Laura?"

She had forgotten her feet. She could walk without limping when she remembered to. She said, "My shoes hurt, Pa."

In the house, Pa sat down and took Carrie on his knee. Then he reached down and felt Laura's shoes.

"Ouch! My toes are tight!" Laura exclaimed.

"I should say they are!" said Pa. "Your feet have grown since last winter. How are yours, Mary?"

Mary said her toes were tight, too.

"Take off your shoes, Mary," said Pa. "And Laura, you put them on."

Mary's shoes did not pinch Laura's feet. They were good shoes, without one rip or hole in them.

"They will look almost like new when I have greased them well," said Pa. "Mary must have new shoes. Laura can wear Mary's, and Laura's shoes can wait for Carrie to grow to them. It won't take her long. Now what else is lacking, Caroline? Think what we need, and we'll get what we can of it. Just as soon as I can hitch up we're all going to town!"

VASILISSA, BABA YAGA, AND THE LITTLE DOLL

"Granny, can you tell me who is the white rider on the white horse, the one who passed at dawn?"

"He is my Bright Morning, and he brings the early light."

"Then who is the rider all in red on the flame-red horse?"

"Ah, he is my Fiery Sun and brings the day."

"And who is the horseman all in black on the coal-black horse?"

"He is my Dark Night. All are my faithful servants. Now I shall ask you a question; mind you answer me properly. How did you do all the tasks I set you?"

A dangerous question! For Baba Yaga, great witch of Russian fairy tale, is also one of the great witches of *all* fairy tale—quite unmistakeable with her hut mounted on hens' claws and her pestle and mortar (a heavy bowl and pounder used by cooks and chemists) for an air-limousine. Only a witch of quality and of rare grim humour would think to fly around in anything so unlikely. But in this splendid story the unnamed doll is her full match in magic! Friend, confidant, solver of problems that seem insoluble, this is the doll of everyone's secret wish.

VASILISSA, BABA YAGA, AND THE LITTLE DOLL

Re-told by Naomi Lewis

In a far-off land in a far-off time, on the edge of a great forest, lived a girl named Vasilissa. Ah, poor Vasilissa! She was no more than eight years old when her mother died. But she had a friend, and that one was better than most. Who was this friend? A doll. As the mother lay ill she had called the child to her bedside. "Vasilissa," she said, "here is a little doll. Take good care of her, and whenever you are in great need, give her some food and ask for her help; she will tell you what to do. Take her, with my blessing; but remember, she is your secret; no one else must know of her at all. Now I can die content."

The father of Vasilissa grieved for a time, then married a new wife, thinking that she would care for the little girl. But did she indeed! She had two daughters of her own, and not one of the three had a grain of love for Vasilissa. From early dawn to the last light of day, in the hot sun or the icy wind, they kept her toiling at all the hardest tasks, in or out of the house; never did she have a word of thanks. Yet whatever they set her to do was done, and done in time. For when she truly needed help she would set her doll on a ledge or table, give her a little food and drink, and tell the doll her troubles. With her help all was done.

One day in the late autumn the father had to leave for the town, a journey of many days. He set off at earliest dawn.

Darkness fell early. Rain beat on the cottage windows; the wind howled down the chimney—just the time for the wife to work a plan she had in mind. To each of the girls she gave a task: the first was set to making lace, the second to knitting stockings, Vasilissa to spinning.

"No stirring from your place, my girls, before you have done," said the woman. Then, leaving them a single candle, she went to bed.

The three worked on for a while, but the light was small, and flickered. One sister pretended to trim the wick and it went out altogether—just as the mother had planned.

"Now we're in trouble," said the girl. "For where's the new light to come from?"

"There's only one place," said her sister, "and that's from Baba Yaga."

"That's right," said the other. "But who's to go?

> *My needles shine;*
> *The job's not mine."*

"I can manage too," said the other.

> *"My lace-pins shine;*
> *the job's not mine.*

Vasilissa must go."

"Yes, Vasilissa must go!" they cried together. And they pushed her out of the door.

Now who was Baba Yaga? She was a mighty witch; her hut was set on claws, like the legs of giant hens. She rode in a mortar over the highest mountains, speeding it on with the pestle, sweeping away her traces with a broom. And she would crunch up in a trice any human who crossed her path.

But Vasilissa had a friend, and that one better than most. She took the doll from her pocket, and set some bread before her. "Little doll," she said, "they are sending me into the forest to fetch a light from Baba Yaga's hut—and who has ever returned from there? Help me, little doll."

The doll ate, and her eyes grew bright as stars. "Have no fear," said she. "While I am with you nothing can do you harm. But remember—no one else must know of your secret. Now let us start."

How dark it was in the forest of towering trees! How the leaves hissed, how the branches creaked and moaned in the wind! But

Vasilissa walked resolutely on, hour after hour. Suddenly, the earth began to tremble and a horseman thundered by. Both horse and rider were glittering white, hair and mane, swirling cloak and bridle too; and as they passed, the sky showed the first white light of dawn.

Vasilissa journeyed on, then again she heard a thundering noise, and a second horse and rider flashed into sight. Both shone red as scarlet, red as flame, swirling cloak and bridle too; as they rode beyond her view, the sun rose high. It was day.

On she walked, on and on, until she reached a clearing in the woods. In the centre was a hut—but the hut had feet; and they were the claws of hens. It was Baba Yaga's home, no doubt about that. All around was a fence of bones, and the posts were topped with skulls: a fearful sight in the fading light! And as she gazed, a third horseman thundered past; but this time horse and rider were black and black, swirling cloak and bridle too. They vanished into the gloom, and it was night. But, as darkness fell, the eyes of the skulls lit up like lamps and everything in the glade could be seen as sharp as day.

Swish! Swoosh! Varoom! Varoom! As Vasilissa stood there, frozen stiff with fear, a terrible noise came from over the forest. The wind screeched, the leaves hissed—Baba Yaga was riding home in her huge mortar, using her pestle as an oar, sweeping away the traces with her broom. At the gate of the hut she stopped and sniffed the air with her long nose.

"Phoo! Phoo! I smell Russian flesh!" she croaked. "Who's there? Out you come!"

Vasilissa took courage, stepped forward and made a low curtsey.

"It is I, Vasilissa. My sisters sent me for a light, since ours went out."

"Oh, so that's it!" said the witch. "I know those girls, and their mother too. Well, nothing's for nothing, as they say; you must work for me for a while, then we'll see about the light." She turned to the hut and sang in a high shrill screech:

> "Open gates! Open gates!
> Baba Yaga waits."

The weird fence opened; the witch seized the girl's arm in her bony fingers and pushed her into the hut. "Now," said she, "get a light from the lamps outside,"—she meant the skulls—"and serve my supper. It's in the oven, and the soup's in the cauldron there." She lay down on a bench while Vasilissa carried the food to the table until she was quite worn out, but she dared not stop. And the witch devoured more than ten strong men could have eaten— whole geese and hens and roasted pigs; loaf after loaf; huge buckets of beer and wine, cider and Russian kvass. At last, all that remained was a crust of bread.

"There's your supper, girl," said the witch. "But you must earn it, mind; I don't like greed. While I'm off tomorrow you must clear out the yard; it hasn't been touched for years, and it quite blocks out the view. Then you must sweep the hut, wash the linen, cook the dinner—and mind you cook enough; I was half-starved tonight. Then—for I'll have no lazybones around—there's another little job. You see that sack? It's full of black beans, wheat and poppy seed, some other things too, I dare say. Sort them out into their separate lots, and if a single one is out of place, woe betide! Into the cauldron you shall go, and I'll crunch you up for breakfast in a trice."

So saying, she lay down by the stove and was instantly fast asleep. Snorrre . . . Snorrre . . . It was a horrible sound.

Vasilissa took the doll from her pocket and gave her the piece of bread. "Little doll," said she. "How am I to do all these tasks? Or even one of them? How can a little doll like you help now? We are lost indeed."

"Vasilissa," said the doll. "Again I tell you, have no fear. Say your prayers and go to sleep. Tomorrow knows what is hidden from yesterday."

She slept—but she woke early, before the first glimmer of day. Where should she start on the mountain of work? Then she heard a thundering of hoofs; white horse and white rider flashed past the window—suddenly it was dawn. The light in the skulls' eyes dwindled and went out. Then the poor girl hid in the shadows, for she saw Baba Yaga get to her feet—Creak! Creak!—and shuffle to the door. There, the witch gave a piercing whistle, and mortar, pestle and broom came hurtling towards her, stopping where she stood. In she stepped, off she rode, over tree-tops, through the clouds, using the pestle like an oar, sweeping away her traces with the broom. Just as she soared away, the red horse and red rider thundered past: suddenly it was day, and the sun shone down.

Vasilissa turned away from the window, but what was this? She could not believe her eyes.

Every task was done. The yard was cleared, the linen washed, the grains and the seeds were all in separate bins, the dinner was set to cook. And there was the little doll, waiting to get back in her pocket. "All you need to do," said the doll, "is to set the table and serve it all, hot and hot, when she returns. But keep your wits about you all the same, for she's a sly one."

The winter daylight faded fast; again there was a thundering of hoofs; black horse, black rider sped through the glade and were gone. Darkness fell, and the eyes of the skulls once more began to glow. And then, with a swish and a roar, down swept the mortar, out stepped Baba Yaga.

"Well, girl, why are you standing idle? You know what I told you."

"The work is all done, granny."

Baba Yaga looked and looked but done it all was. So she sat down, grumbling and mumbling, to eat her supper. It was good, very good: it put her in a pleasant humour, for a witch.

"Tell me, girl, why do you sit there as if you were dumb?"

"Granny, I did not dare to speak—but, now, if you permit it, may I ask a question?"

"Ask if you will, but remember that not every question leads to good. The more you know, the older you grow."

"Well, granny, can you tell me, who is the white rider on the white horse, the one who passed at dawn?"

"He is my Bright Morning, and he brings the earliest light."

"Then who is the rider all in red on the flame-red horse?"

"Ah, he is my Fiery Sun and brings the day."

"And who is the horseman all in black on the coal-black horse?"

"He is my Dark Night. All are my faithful servants. Now I shall ask *you* a question; mind you answer me properly. How did you do all those tasks I set you?"

Vasilissa recalled her mother's words, never to tell the secret of the doll.

"My mother gave me a blessing before she died, and that helps me when in need."

"A blessing! I want no blessed children here! Out you get! Away! Away!" And she pushed her through the door. "You've earned your pay—now take it." She took down one of the gatepost skulls, fixed it on a stick, and thrust it into Vasilissa's hand. "Now—off!"

Vasilissa needed no second bidding. She hastened on, her path

ST. DANIEL'S CHURCH
7007 Holcomb Road
Box 171
Clarkston, Michigan 48016

now lit by the eyes of the fearful lamp. And so, at last, she was home.

"Why have you taken so long?" screamed the mother and the sisters. They had been in darkness ever since she left. They had gone in every direction to borrow a light, but once it was inside in the house, every flame went out. So they seized the skull with joy.

But the glaring eyes stared back; wherever they turned they could not escape the scorching rays. Soon, all that remained of the three was a little ash. Then the light of the skull went out for ever; its task was done.

Vasilissa buried it in the garden, and a bush of red roses sprang up on the spot. She did not fear to be alone, for the little doll kept her company. And when her father returned, rejoicing to see her, this tale she told him, just as it has been told to you.

ST. DAVID'S CHURCH
2700 Holcomb
Box 171
Dearborn, Michigan 48124

THE DUMB SOLDIER

I shall find him, never fear
I shall find my grenadier . . .

This poem is from *A Child's Garden of Verses*, first published in
1885, and still perhaps the best of all books of poems for and about
young children, in English at any rate. Stevenson (1850–94) was
often ill during his rather lonely childhood in Edinburgh but
(very much like Andersen) did immense adventuring through
toys, books, leaves on the water, anything really—look through
the poems and you can see for yourself. He knew Andersen's
stories (he mentions Gerda and Kay in another poem), and he
must have read *The Steadfast Tin Soldier*. Could it have given him
the idea of sending his own steadfast soldier on a strange and
magical adventure that, as a human child, he could never under-
take himself?

THE DUMB SOLDIER

Robert Louis Stevenson

When the grass was closely mown,
Walking on the lawn alone
In the turf a hole I found
And hid a soldier underground.

Spring and daisies came apace;
Grasses hid my hiding place;
Grasses ran like a green sea
O'er the lawn up to my knee.

Under grass alone he lies,
Looking up with leaden eyes,
Scarlet coat and pointed gun,
To the stars and to the sun.

When the grass is ripe like grain,
When the scythe is stoned again,
When the lawn is shaven clear,
Then my hole shall reappear.

I shall find him, never fear.
I shall find my grenadier;
But for all that's gone and come,
I shall find my soldier dumb.

He has lived, a little thing;
In the grassy woods of spring;
Done, if he could tell me true,
Just as I should like to do.

He has seen the starry hours
And the springing of the flowers;
And the fairy things that pass
In the forests of the grass.

In the silence he has heard
Talking bee and ladybird,
And the butterfly has flown
O'er him as he lay alone

Not a word will he disclose,
Not a word of all he knows,
I must lay him on the shelf
And make up the tale myself.

RAG BAG

Silently, out of nothing at all, a queer little person gradually took shape. She was a small child, but her white face was not child-like. Her clothes were not suitable for a child either. They seemed to be a bundle of dark rags . . . She was not of this world.

"Go away!" said Carol. "Please go back where you came from and don't visit us again. Not ever."

The queer child gathered up her dark, trailing skirt and ran away nimbly on bare feet . . .

An unusual story, this, about a fairy child who envies the pleasure that a human child gets from her dolls and wants one of them for herself. It's a tale about different kinds of magic, really. What the eerie, pathetic but rather stupid fairy lacks, and Carol (a nicer human child than some) possesses is the one sort of magic granted to humans (or some of them, and even then not used nearly enough)—imagination.

RAG BAG

Ruth Ainsworth

CAROL was playing halfway up the stairs. She was sitting on one stair, and on the next stair up she had spread out three little blue cups and three little blue saucers and three little blue plates. Also a milk jug and a sugar bowl. On the next step up, above the tea set, sat her three dolls, their legs stuck stiffly out and their faces smiling with anticipation.

There was Rag Bag, the oldest doll, who had belonged to Carol's mother, and before that to her grandmother. Her looks were not improved by the many adventures she had had in her long life, but all the hugs and kisses she had had gave her face a contented expression. She was dearly loved and loved everybody else in return.

The next was Saucy Sally, a very smart doll with fashionable clothes. She had real hair and black patent slippers. She carried a handbag which closed with a zip.

The third doll was a boy called Jolly Roger, or Roger for short. He had a sailor hat on the back of his curly head and a sailor's blouse with a wide collar. He had flappy blue trousers and gold ear-rings in his ears.

Carol loved all her dolls but she had a special feeling for Rag Bag because she could do something the others couldn't manage. She could speak, though she only spoke when alone with Carol

and the other dolls, never in front of any grown-up person. And no one could call her really talkative. She simply spoke if she had something to say.

"Here is your tea, Rag Bag. Plenty of milk, just as you like it."

Rag Bag's smile spread even further.

"And here is yours, Saucy Sally. Three lumps of sugar."

Saucy Sally gave a small polite bow.

"And here is yours, Roger. A good strong cup for a sturdy sailor boy."

Roger took his cup and saluted.

"Butter fingers!" said Carol, as the cup tilted. "How you manage on board ship with the deck tilting beats me." Then the food was handed round. Rag Bag took a piece of bread-and-butter, as she had been taught. Saucy Sally bit daintily into a doughnut. Roger took a ship's biscuit. He made dreadful crunching noises, but if you have ever eaten a ship's biscuit you'll know that he couldn't help it. They are so very, very hard. Roger kept looking over his shoulder, so he made a lot of crumbs on the carpet.

"Roger," said Carol, watching him, "have you seen something? Has she appeared again?"

Roger nodded. The others turned their heads too and looked back up the stairs.

"She seems to have gone," said Carol. "That's a good thing."

The dolls looked relieved and went on eating, but Carol kept watch on the landing above, out of the corner of her eye.

Silently, out of nothing at all, a queer little person gradually took shape. She was a small child, but her white face was not child-like. Her clothes were not suitable for a child either. They seemed to be a bundle of dark rags. She had a large, lumpy nose and a very round chin. She was not of this world.

"Go away!" said Carol. "Please go back where you came from and don't visit us again. Not ever."

The queer child gathered up her dark, trailing skirt and ran away nimbly on bare feet.

Carol's voice was shaky with fear, but she comforted the dolls as well as she could.

"I think it must be one of the Little People, or rather one of their children, who has got into the house by mistake. We've seen her three times, haven't we? Looking through the window. Peering into the pram. And rummaging in the toy box."

"This makes four," said Carol, speaking for Roger.

The next time Carol saw anything strange, she was alone in the hall and came face to face with the bundly child. It was no good saying go away. The Fairy Child stood firm. She was not going to budge.

"Do you want something?" said Carol at last.

"Yes, I do. And if you don't give it to me, I'll take it."

"What is it?"

"It's a doll. We Fairy Children don't have dolls. I'll have one of yours."

"You can't. I can't spare one. They are mine. I'll make you a doll. Come tomorrow and she'll be ready."

Carol had an older sister called Kate, and Kate helped her to make a doll, or she could never have managed alone.

"What do you want another doll *for*?" asked Kate.

"For a sort of present. A secret present," explained Carol.

The doll was made out of a clothes' peg, with one side of the head blacked with shoe polish for hair, and a face drawn on the other side. Kate made a shawl out of a handkerchief and a skirt out of an egg cosy.

"Will she do?" asked Kate, holding her at arm's length.

"She'll do beautifully. Thank you, Kate," said Carol.

The next day the Fairy Child appeared, suddenly and silently, as usual.

"Where is my doll?" she inquired abruptly.

"Here," said Carol, handing her over. "Be kind to her."

"She'll do," said the Fairy Child, ungraciously.

"Don't please come back," begged Carol.

"I might!" said the Child with a teasing laugh.

Carol and her dolls were left in peace for some days and they began to feel safe and comfortable, and stopped looking in dark corners and behind things. Then, on a Saturday morning, the Fairy Child appeared again, with no warning. One minute she wasn't there. The next minute she was. She came close to Carol and caught hold of her arm. Carol felt the chill of her sharp fingers through her jersey.

"I want a handbag for my doll."

Saucy Sally moved behind Rag Bag, hiding her handbag. Roger was shaking so much his ear-rings jingled.

"I'll try to make one, if you give me time," said Carol.

"Tomorrow?" asked the Child. "I don't like waiting."

"Tomorrow, then," said Carol doubtfully.

Once more she had to ask Kate to help her, but this time Kate was not so willing to help. She was keeping a diary and drawing a picture to illustrate every day, and that took most of her leisure. But she realized that Carol was upset about something and she said she would have a go at making a handbag.

In the end, Kate cut the thumb off an old glove and tied a piece of ribbon round the mouth for a handle. Then they added a drop of their mother's scent.

The next day the Fairy Child appeared. She did not think much of the handbag, but she liked the scent, and went off sniffing and grumbling.

Once more there was peace in the house, but not for long. The unwelcome visitor came again, swinging her doll carelessly, and this time she asked, indeed demanded, "ear-rings for my doll".

Roger, very conscious of his ear-rings, crept under the table and pretended he wasn't there.

"I could draw some on with my coloured pens," suggested Carol. "What colour would you like?"

"That wouldn't do at all. They must swing and jingle. If you can't make me a proper doll I shall have to take one of yours. You can surely spare *one*."

"Well, I can't. They are my children. Could your mother spare one of her children?"

"I expect she could. She has ten other children and she can't

count beyond double figures. It's a family failing. She'd never know I'd gone."

"Then I'm not like your mother," replied Carol. "But I'll see what I can do. You'll have to leave her with me till tomorrow. I'll take great care of her."

"She's very tough," said the Fairy Child, handing the peg doll over upside down. "She'll come to no harm. She gets more kicks than kisses. I pinch her much more often than I pet her."

"You don't deserve to have a doll if you don't know how to treat her!" Carol's eyes filled with tears as she cradled the little peg doll in her arms. "Kicks indeed," she muttered. "I'd like to kick you."

"I heard what you whispered," said the Fairy Child, "and I shan't forget it. We Little People have good ears and good memories."

Carol knew that even Kate would be no help in making earrings but her father might be able to do something. He had a tool box full of all kinds of tools. When he came home she asked him:

"Daddy. Can you make ear-rings for a doll?"

"I could try, I suppose. Where's the doll?"

Carol gave him the little peg doll.

"I'll have to drill two holes and the wood might split. Keep your fingers crossed. I'll have a go when I've had my tea."

The wood didn't split and by bedtime the peg doll was wearing wire ear-rings that looked like silver and jingled when she shook her head.

Next time the bundly Child appeared, Carol's three dolls hid themselves in the toy box. There was no telling what she would take a fancy to next, Roger's anchor buttons or Saucy Sally's shiny shoes. Only Rag Bag was not worried. She was so old and shabby that no one would take any notice of her.

The Fairy Child jingled the new ear-rings. Remarked that she would have preferred gold. Scowled at Carol, and disappeared.

"Perhaps we've seen the last of her," sighed Carol.

"Don't be too sure," said Rag Bag. "But whatever happens we'll get the better of her. We'll use our brains."

"Perhaps she has a good brain as well as a good memory?"

"Anyhow, she hasn't a heart. More pinching than petting, indeed."

The other dolls looked shocked. What a dreadful place the world seemed, beyond the walls of their safe, warm home, where they only knew kindness and gentle voices.

Weeks passed and there was no visit from the Fairy Child. Saucy Sally and Roger forgot all about her, but Rag Bag never

forgot, though she kept her thoughts to herself. Carol sometimes
shuddered when an unexpected shadow fell on her path. Then,
one dull day in the garden, she found the Fairy Child was standing
at her side. At first neither of them spoke.

"How is your doll?" asked Carol. "What have you called her?"

"Oh, that wooden peg creature." The Fairy Child laughed
unpleasantly. "I got tired of her. I threw her in the dustbin."

"But why? She was so nice with her ear-rings and her smile and
everything."

"Nice! I don't call her nice. I call her a stupid wooden image.

She couldn't talk or sing or dance or eat or amuse me. She was useless."

"Couldn't you pretend she could do all those things? I pretend my dolls can do anything in the world. They can even fly, if I want them to."

"I never pretend. I don't know how to pretend. I don't want a doll if I have to pretend things. I want a real companion who can do everything that I can do. I want one of *your* dolls."

"But if you had one of my dolls," said Carol, "you'd still have to pretend. So you wouldn't be better pleased than you were with the peg doll."

"I don't believe you," said the Fairy Child angrily. "I've seen you having fun with your dolls—giving parties—having adventures. I often hear other voices beside yours. A very high voice and a very gruff voice. I know one is Sally and one is Roger. You aren't speaking the truth. They can do lots of things my stupid peg doll couldn't. That's why I threw her in the dustbin."

Carol opened her eyes in amazement. "But don't you understand," she explained. "It's all pretending. I speak in a high voice for Sally and a gruff one for Roger. It all seems real, but I'm only playing. Only pretending."

"I don't believe you," said the Fairy Child stubbornly.

Carol was very thankful that Rag Bag hadn't been mentioned because she really could speak. There was the sound of footsteps approaching.

"I shall come back tomorrow and make my choice," said the Fairy Child, fading into a bush. "And it's no good trying to hide them because I shall find them. I can see through things."

"I thought I heard voices," said Carol's mother coming along the path.

"I was playing," said Carol quickly, "with Rag Bag."

"I'm so glad you like Rag Bag," said her mother. "I loved her when I was your age, and so did granny who had her first. She's such a comfortable creature."

"Did she ever talk to you when you were little?" asked Carol.

"What a strange question to ask. I know I pretended she could talk. It's so long ago, but I almost think she did. But she couldn't, could she?"

"I don't see why not," said Carol, giving Rag Bag a hug.

At bedtime, Rag Bag was nowhere to be seen. She always slept with Carol, snug in her arms with her head sharing the pillow, her bright yellow locks, which were getting thin with age, mixed with Carol's brown hair.

"How awful if that horrible child has stolen her away," said Carol, almost in tears.

"She said 'tomorrow'," comforted Roger.

"And she usually does what she says," added Saucy Sally.

Just then, Rag Bag appeared, out of breath as she had been running. The pockets of her apron were bulging with rowan berries. Her feet were wet.

"Where ever have you been?" asked Carol.

"I've been in the garden, preparing for the worst," said Rag Bag, climbing into bed, wet feet and bulging pockets and all.

During the night, Rag Bag freed herself very slowly and

carefully from Carol's arms and crept out of bed. She spent a long time sitting on the floor in the moonlight, Carol's work basket beside her, busy with a needle and a long length of thread. When she had finished what she was doing she tidied the work basket, put the lid on, and crept back into Carol's warm bed.

The next day, no one could settle to anything. Carol started every time there was an unexpected sound, and if a door banged, or someone sneezed, the dolls dived behind curtains.

When the Fairy Child appeared, no one was expecting her. She just grew up out of the floor, suddenly and silently, like a mushroom. No one ran away or tried to hide. They all kept still as stones.

"I said I'd be here today and here I am," she said in her disagreeable voice. "I've decided to have Rag Bag. I know there's something special about her and I mean to find out what it is. There's some mystery I don't understand."

"You can't. I love her so much. I've always had her since I was a baby." Carol was almost crying.

"Then it's time someone else had a turn. Come on, Rag Bag."

Carol snatched Rag Bag up in her arms, but Rag Bag whispered in her ear:

"Let me go. I'll come back. Trust me and don't fret."

Carol slowly let go and the Fairy Child took her remarkably gently in her arms and they vanished through the door without opening it.

"We must be brave," said Carol in a shaky voice. "Rag Bag said she'd come back and so she will. Let's play snakes and ladders to cheer ourselves up. You can have first turn, Roger."

"Where are you taking me?" asked Rag Bag as the Fairy Child hurried along, still holding her gently.

"To the Fairy Hill where you'll spend the rest of your life. So you *can* talk, after all. You can talk perfectly. Carol was telling lies."

"No, she wasn't telling lies," said Rag Bag indignantly. "She said Saucy Sally and Roger couldn't talk and they can't. Not a word. She has to talk for them."

"Then why is it you can talk? Tell me that."

"I was made by a wise old woman who stitched some magic into me," said Rag Bag. "And it's still there."

"I wish you could walk as well. My arms are aching."

"Then why not have a rest?" said Rag Bag.

"I will. You can tell me a story."

"All right," agreed Rag Bag.

The Fairy Child lay down under a tree, because they were passing through a wood, and closed her eyes. Rag Bag began a very uninteresting story about two bears called Nid and Nod. Soon the Fairy Child was fast asleep.

Then Rag Bag worked quickly. First she whispered a sleep charm into the Fairy Child's ear to make sure that she would not wake for a long time.

> "*Sleep, sleep,*
> *Deep, deep,*
> *Count a thousand sheep*
> *Into the fold.*"

She repeated this three times. Then she took out of her apron pocket the long, long string of rowan berries that she had threaded during the night. She laid the string in a circle round the sleeping Child. Then she set off home. She might easily have lost the way, but every creature in the wood helped her.

"Over here, over here," squeaked a mouse.

"That way, that way," whistled a bird.

"Over the log, over the log," snuffled a hedgehog.

"Cross the stream, cross the stream," croaked a frog.

So she found her way safely and easily, and ended up in her own garden. Carol was sitting on the swing with the dolls in her lap. The swing was just moving. All three looked the picture of misery.

"She said she'd come back," said Roger trying to sound comforting. "She'll come in the end."

"But I want her now. This very minute," said Carol. "Oh Rag Bag, why did I let you go so easily? There must have been something I could have done."

"Well, here I am, just as I said," and Rag Bag climbed on to Carol's lap with the other two. They all hugged and kissed each other, and when Rag Bag could speak, she related her adventures. She described how she had gathered the rowan berries and threaded them into a long string, because the Fairy Folk hate and fear the rowan tree and its fruits.

"When the Fairy Child wakes up," went on Rag Bag, "she won't be able to move. She won't dare to cross the rowan berry ring."

"Will she starve to death?" asked Carol. "I feel sorry for her."

"Oh no," said Rag Bag. "Some of her own people will find her and they'll discover a way of moving the berries without actually touching them. Then she'll be free. But I shall be surprised if she shows her face here again. She'll have had such a fright."

That night, when they were all in bed, Carol asked Rag Bag to tell them the sleepy story about Nid and Nod because they were far too excited to go to sleep. Rag Bag began it and it was so very dull that everyone was asleep in no time. Then, just to make sure, she whispered the sleep charm:

> "*Sleep, sleep,*
> *Deep, deep.*
> *Count a thousand sheep*
> *Into the fold.*"

ROCKING-HORSE LAND

The moon was shining in through the window making a square cistern of light upon the floor. And then, all at once, he saw that the rocking-horse had moved from the place where he had left it! It had crossed the room, and was standing close to the window with its head towards the night . . .

Wild-eyed, restless, moving with urgent energy yet held in the same place, the rocking-horse always suggests the need for escape and for soaring flight, a need which is exactly caught in this fine mysterious tale. Laurence Housman, younger brother of A. E. Housman who wrote *A Shropshire Lad*, lived for nearly a century (1865–1959), had several professions, and was something of a romantic rebel, supporting such causes as the Suffragettes and the League of Nations well before these ideas were generally fashionable. He began as an artist and illustrator, became Art Critic of the *Manchester Guardian*, and then realised that writing was much more to his taste and skill. His great success came in the 1920s and '30s, with two groups of short plays, one group about St Francis, the other about Queen Victoria and various eminent contemporaries seen in their private lives.

But his earliest writings (between 1894 and 1905) were fairy tales of a haunting, melodious charm, and *Rocking-Horse Land* is one of them. If it seems to have a flavour very much like one of Wilde's resounding fairy tales this is hardly surprising, for it belongs to the same mood and period.

ROCKING-HORSE LAND

Laurence Housman

LITTLE Prince Freedling woke up with a jump, and sprang out of bed into the sunshine. He was five years old that morning, by all the clocks and calendars in the kingdom; and the day was going to be beautiful. Every golden minute was precious. He was dressed and out of the room before the attendants knew that he was awake.

In the ante-chamber stood piles on piles of glittering presents; when he walked among them they came up to the measure of his waist. His fairy godmother had sent him a toy with the most humorous effect. It was labelled, "Break me and I shall turn into something else." So every time he broke it he got a new toy more beautiful than the last. It began by being a hoop, and from that it ran on, while the Prince broke it incessantly for the space of one hour, during which it became by turn—a top, a Noah's ark, a skipping-rope, a man-of-war, a box of bricks, a picture puzzle, a pair of stilts, a drum, a trumpet, a kaleidoscope, a steam-engine, and nine hundred and fifty other things exactly. Then he began to grow discontented, because it would never turn into the same thing again; and after having broken the man-of-war he wanted to get it back again. Also he wanted to see if the steam-engine would go inside the Noah's ark; but the toy would never be two things at the same time either. This was very unsatisfactory. He thought his fairy godmother ought to have sent him two toys, out of which he could make combinations.

At last he broke it once more, and it turned into a kite; and while he was flying the kite he broke the string, and the kite went sailing away up into the nasty blue sky, and was never heard of again.

Then Prince Freedling sat down and howled at his fairy godmother; what a dissembling lot fairy godmothers were, to be sure! They were always setting traps to make their god-children unhappy. Nevertheless, when told to, he took up his pen and

wrote her a nice little note, full of bad spelling and tarradiddles, to say what a happy birthday he was spending in breaking up the beautiful toy she had sent him.

Then he went to look at the rest of the presents, and found it quite refreshing to break a few that did not send him giddy by turning into anything else.

Suddenly his eyes became fixed with delight; alone, right at the end of the room, stood a great black rocking-horse. The saddle and bridle were hung with tiny gold bells and balls of coral; and the horse's tail and mane flowed till they almost touched the ground.

The Prince scampered across the room, and threw his arms around the beautiful creature's neck. All its bells jingled as the head swayed gracefully down; and the prince kissed it between the eyes. Great eyes they were, the colour of fire, so wonderfully bright, it seemed they must be really alive, only they did not move, but gazed continually with a set stare at the tapestry hung walls on which were figures of armed knights riding to battle.

So Prince Freedling mounted to the back of his rocking-horse; and all day long he rode and shouted to the figures of the armed knights, challenging them to fight, or leading them against the enemy.

At length, when it came to be bedtime, weary of so much glory, he was lifted down from the saddle and carried away to bed.

In his sleep Freedling still felt his black rocking-horse swinging to and fro under him, and heard the melodious chime of its bells, and, in the land of dreams, saw a great country open before him, full of the sound of the battle-cry and the hunting horn calling him to strange perils and triumphs.

In the middle of the night he grew softly awake, and his heart was full of love for his black rocking-horse. He crept gently out of bed: he would go and look at it where it was standing so grand and still in the next room, to make sure it was all safe and not afraid of being by itself in the dark night. Parting the door-hangings he passed through into the wide hollow chamber beyond, all littered about with toys.

The moon was shining in through the window, making a square cistern of light upon the floor. And then, all at once, he saw that the rocking-horse had moved from the place where he had left it! It had crossed the room, and was standing close to the window, with its head toward the night, as though watching the movement of the clouds and the trees swaying in the wind.

The Prince could not understand how it had been moved so; he was a little bit afraid, and stealing timidly across, he took hold of the bridle to comfort himself with the jangle of its bells. As he came close, and looked up into the dark solemn face he saw that the eyes were full of tears, and reaching up felt one fall warm against his hand.

"Why do you weep, my Beautiful?" said the Prince.

The rocking-horse answered, "I weep because I am a prisoner, and not free. Open the window, Master, and let me go!"

"But if I let you go I shall lose you," said the Prince. "Cannot you be happy here with me?"

"Let me go," said the horse, "for my brothers call me out of

Rocking-Horse Land; I hear my mare whinnying to her foals; and they all cry, seeking me through the ups and hollows of my native fastnesses! Sweet Master, let me go this night, and I will return to you when it is day!"

Then Freedling said, "How shall I know that you will return: and what name shall I call you by?"

And the rocking-horse answered. "My name is Rollonde. Search my mane till you find in it a white hair; draw it out and wind it upon one of your fingers; and so long as you have it so wound you are my master; and wherever I am I must return at your bidding."

So the Prince drew down the rocking-horse's head, and searching the mane, he found the white hair, and wound it upon his finger and tied it. Then he kissed Rollonde between the eyes, saying, "Go, Rollonde, since I love you, and wish you to be happy; only return to me when it is day!" And so saying, he threw open the window to the stir of the night.

Then the rocking-horse lifted his dark head and neighed aloud for joy, and swaying forward with a mighty circling motion rose full into the air, and sprang out into the free world before him.

Freedling watched how with plunge and curve he went over the bowed trees; and again he neighed into the darkness of the night, then swifter than wind he disappeared in the distance. And faintly from far away came a sound of the neighing of many horses answering him.

Then the Prince closed the window and crept back to bed:

and all night long he he dreamed strange dreams of Rocking-Horse Land. There he saw smooth hills and valleys that rose and sank without a stone or a tree to disturb the steel-like polish of their surface, slippery as glass, and driven over by a strong wind; and over them, with a sound like the humming of bees, flew the rocking-horses. Up and down, up and down, with bright manes streaming like coloured fires, and feet motionless behind and before, went the swift pendulum of their flight. Their long bodies bowed and rose; their heads worked to give impetus to their going; they cried, neighing to each other over hill and valley, "Which of us shall be first? Which of us shall be first? After them the mares with their tall foals came spinning to watch, crying also among themselves, "Ah! which shall be first?"

"Rollonde, Rollonde is first!" shouted the Prince, clapping his hands as they reached the goal; and at that, all at once, he woke and saw it was broad day. Then he ran and threw open the window, and holding out the finger that carried the white hair, cried, "Rollonde, Rollonde, come back, Rollonde!"

Far away he heard an answering sound; and in another moment there came the great rocking-horse himself, dipping and dancing over the hills. He crossed the woods and cleared the palace-wall at a bound, and floating in through the window, dropped to rest at Prince Freedling's side, rocking gently to and fro as though panting from the strain of his long flight.

"Now are you happy?" asked the Prince as he caressed him.

"Ah! sweet Prince," said Rollonde, "ah, kind Master!" And then he said no more, but became the still staring rocking-horse of the day before, with fixed eyes and rigid limbs, which could do nothing but rock up and down with a jangling of sweet bells so long as the Prince rode him.

That night Freedling came again when all was still in the palace; and now as before Rollonde had moved from his place and was standing with his head against the window waiting to be let out. "Ah, dear Master," he said, so soon as he saw the Prince coming, "let me go this night also, and surely I will return with day."

So again the Prince opened the window, and watched him disappear, and heard from far away the neighing of the horses in Rocking-Horse Land calling to him. And in the morning with the white hair round his finger he called "Rollonde, Rollonde!" and Rollonde neighed and came back to him, dipping and dancing over the hills.

Now this same thing happened every night; and every morning the horse kissed Freedling, saying, "Ah! dear Prince and kind Master," and became stock still once more.

So a year went by, till one morning Freedling woke up to find it was his sixth birthday. And as six is to five, so were the presents he received on his sixth birthday for magnificence and multitude to the presents he had received the year before. His fairy godmother had sent him a bird, a real live bird; but when he pulled its tail it became a lizard, and when he pulled the lizard's tail it became a mouse, and when he pulled the mouse's tail it became a cat. Then he did very much want to see if the cat would eat the mouse, and not being able to have them both he got rather vexed with his fairy godmother. However, he pulled the cat's tail and the cat became a dog, and when he pulled the dog's tail the dog became a goat; and so it went on till he got to a cow. And he pulled the cow's tail and it became a camel, and he pulled the camel's tail and it became an elephant, and still not being contented, he pulled the elephant's tail and it became a guinea-pig. Now a guinea-pig has no tail to pull, so it remained a guinea-pig, while Prince Freedling sat down and howled at his fairy godmother.

But the best of all his presents was the one given to him by the King, his father. It was a most beautiful horse, for, said the King, "You are now old enough to learn to ride."

So Freedling was put upon the horse's back and from having ridden so long upon his rocking-horse he learned to ride perfectly in a single day, and was declared by all the courtiers to be the most perfect equestrian that was ever seen.

Now these praises and the pleasure of riding a real horse so occupied his thoughts that that night he forgot all about Rollonde,

and falling fast asleep dreamed of nothing but real horses and horsemen going to battle. And so it was the next night too.

But the night after that, just as he was falling asleep, he heard someone sobbing by his bed, and a voice saying, "Ah! dear Prince and kind Master, let me go for my heart breaks for a sight of my native land." And there stood his poor rocking-horse Rollonde, with tears falling out of his beautiful eyes on to the white coverlet.

Then the Prince, full of shame at having forgotten his friend, sprang up and threw his arms round his neck saying, "Be of good cheer, Rollonde, for now surely I will let thee go!" and he ran to the window and opened it for the horse to go through. "Ah, dear Prince and kind Master!" said Rollonde. Then he lifted his head and neighed so that the whole palace shook, and swaying forward till his head almost touched the ground he sprang out into the night and away towards Rocking-Horse Land.

Then Prince Freedling, standing by the window, thoughtfully unloosed the white hair from his finger, and let it float away into the darkness, out of sight of his eye or reach of his hand.

"Good-bye, Rollonde," he murmured softly, "brave Rollonde, my own good Rollonde! Go and be happy in your own land, since I, your Master, was forgetting to be kind to you." And far away he heard the neighing of horses in Rocking-Horse Land.

Many years after, when Freedling had become King in his father's stead, the fifth birthday of the Prince his son came to be celebrated; and there on the morning of the day, among all the

presents that covered the floor of the chamber stood a beautiful
foal rocking-horse, black, with deep-burning eyes.

No one knew how it had come there, or whose present it was,
till the King himself came to look at it. And when he saw it so like
the old Rollonde he had loved as a boy, he smiled, and, stroking
its dark mane, said softly in its ear, "Art thou, then, the son of
Rollonde?" And the foal answered him, "Ah, dear Prince and
kind Master!" but never a word more.

Then the King took the little Prince his son, and told him the
story of Rollonde as I have told it here; and at the end he went
and searched in the foal's mane till he found one white hair, and
drawing it out, he wound it about the little Prince's finger,
bidding him guard it well and be ever a kind master to Rollonde's
son.

ELIZABETH

"What's its name?" asked Kate.

"She doesn't have a name," Kate's mother said. "No one has a name until somebody loves her."

Kate set the doll back in the box. "Thank you," she said to her mother politely. "It's an ugly doll," she said to herself inside. "It's an ugly doll and I hate it very much."

An excellent story, perfectly demonstrating the true child-doll, doll-child relationship. Where it works, both acquire a kind of magic. Where it does not—well . . . (You can see this too in the tale.) The mother—unlike some of the adults in these stories—clearly understands doll-nature. "What does it do?" the child asks grumpily. "Everything a doll's supposed to do," is the answer. Discovering that is this tale's surprise and triumph. It could hardly have been better told.

ELIZABETH

Liesel Moak Skorpen

"WHAT do you want for Christmas?" asked Kate's mother.

"I want a red ball," said Kate, "and a new dress and a book and a doll. I want a doll with golden curls who walks and talks and turns somersaults."

"Well," said Kate's mother, "we shall see what surprises Christmas brings."

It seemed as though Christmas would never come, but of course Christmas came. Kate opened her presents under the tree. There was a red ball and a new dress and a book and other gifts. And underneath them all, in a long white box, there was a doll. It was a soft cloth doll with warm brown eyes and thick brown plaits like Kate's.

"What does it do?" asked Kate.

"Everything a doll's supposed to do," her mother said.

Kate picked the doll up from its box. Its arms hung limply at its sides. Its weak legs flopped, and they couldn't hold it up. "What's its name?" asked Kate.

"She doesn't have a name," Kate's mother said. "No one has a name until somebody loves her."

Kate set the doll back in the box. "Thank you," she said to her mother politely. "It's an ugly doll," she said to herself inside. "It's an ugly doll, and I hate it very much."

There were no more presents under the tree.

Kate's cousin Agnes came for Christmas dinner. Agnes had a new doll whose name was Charlotte Louise. Charlotte Louise could walk and talk. "Where is your Christmas doll?" asked Agnes.

Kate showed her the cloth doll lying in the box.

"What does it do?" asked Agnes.

"It doesn't do anything," Kate replied.

"What is its name?" asked Agnes.

"It doesn't have a name," said Kate.

"It certainly is an ugly doll," said Agnes. She set Charlotte Louise down on the floor, and Charlotte Louise turned a somersault.

"I hate you, Agnes," Kate said, "and I hate your ugly doll!"

Kate was sent upstairs to bed without any Christmas cake.

The next day was the day after Christmas. Kate's mother asked her to put away her presents. Kate put away her red ball and her new dress and her book and all her other gifts except the doll.

"I don't want this ugly doll," she said to James the collie. "You may have it if you like."

James wagged his tail. He took the cloth doll in his mouth and carried it out to the snowy garden.

By lunchtime James hadn't come home, and Kate was sorry she had given her doll to him. She couldn't eat her sandwich or her cake. "James will chew up that doll," she said to herself. "He'll chew and chew until there's nothing left but stuffing and some rags. He'll bury her somewhere in the snow."

She put on her coat and mittens and boots and went out into the garden. James was nowhere to be seen. "I'm sorry," said Kate inside herself. "I'm very, very sorry, and I want to find my doll."

Kate looked all over the garden before she found her. The doll was lying under the cherry tree, half-buried in the snow, but except for being wet and cold, she seemed as good as new. Kate brushed her clean and cradled her in her arms. "It's all right now, Elizabeth," she said, "because I love you after all."

Elizabeth could do everything.

When Kate was happy, Elizabeth was happy.

When Kate was sad, Elizabeth understood.

When Kate was naughty and had to go upstairs, Elizabeth went with her.

Elizabeth didn't care for baths. "She doesn't like water," Kate explained, "because of being buried in the snow." Elizabeth sat on the edge of the bath and kept Kate company while she scrubbed.

Elizabeth loved to swing and slide and go round and round on the merry-go-round.

When Kate wanted to be the mother, Elizabeth was the baby.

When Kate wanted to be Cinderella, Elizabeth was a wicked stepsister and the fairy godmother too.

Sometimes Kate forgot about Elizabeth because she was playing with other friends.

Elizabeth waited patiently. When Kate came back, Elizabeth was always glad to see her.

In the spring, Elizabeth and Kate picked violets for Kate's mother's birthday and helped Kate's father fly a kite.

In the summer, everyone went to the seaside. Agnes was there too, but Agnes's doll, Charlotte Louise, was not.

"Where is Charlotte Louise?" Kate asked, holding Elizabeth in her arms.

"Charlotte Louise is broken," Agnes said. "We threw her in the dustbin. I shall have a new doll for Christmas."

Agnes wouldn't go into the water. She was afraid. But Kate went in for a dip. She set Elizabeth on a towel to sleep safely in the sun. When she came out of the water, Elizabeth was gone.

"Help," cried Kate, "please, somebody help! Elizabeth is drowning!"

Everyone heard the word "drowning", but nobody quite heard who. Grown-ups shouted and ran around pointing their fingers towards the sea.

> Then out of nowhere
> Like a streak,
> Galloping, galloping,
> James the collie came.

Out into the sea and back to shore he swam, Elizabeth hanging limply from his mouth.

After an hour in the sun, Elizabeth was as good as new.

Everyone except Agnes said that James was brave and good and a hero.

Kate didn't say that Agnes had thrown Elizabeth into the sea, but inside herself she thought that Agnes had.

In the autumn, Elizabeth helped Kate gather berries in the meadow for jams and jellies and berry pies.

Then Christmas came again. Of course there were presents under the tree. For Kate, there was a new sledge and a new dress and a book and other gifts. For Elizabeth, there was a woollen coat and hat, and two dresses, one of them velvet.

Agnes came for Christmas dinner. Agnes had a new doll whose name was Tina Marie.

"Tina Marie can sing songs," said Agnes. "She can blow bubbles too, and crawl along the floor."

Kate held Elizabeth tightly in her arms. "Well," said Kate in a whisper, "Tina Marie is the ugliest doll I ever saw. She is almost as ugly as you."

Agnes kicked Kate sharply on the leg and said the most dreadful things to Elizabeth, who was looking particularly nice in her velvet dress.

Agnes's mother was very cross with Agnes.

Agnes spent the rest of the day in disgrace and wasn't permitted any Christmas cake.

"Merry Christmas, Elizabeth," said Kate as she tucked her into bed, "and Happy Birthday too! You are the best and most beautiful doll in the world, and I wouldn't swop you for anyone else."

THE MAGIC CHILD

"I feel sure that the doll once belonged to some great family and was much loved . . . for I feel that in some way Tokutaro is more than wood and plaster. Have we not heard how these figures acquire a soul if they are tenderly loved?"

A Japanese fairy tale of great delicacy and charm. The idea—a wanted child arriving in some strange way—appears in legend and story everywhere (Thumbelina, Hans My Hedgehog—how many can you add to this list?). But the doll version is not often found. Tokutaro is of course a real dream-child—always beautiful, always young, always loving, silent except in emergencies and though in the end "never seen again familiarly among men" he still returns to tend the graves of his parents: the ultimate dream-child, the ultimate loved doll.

THE MAGIC CHILD

Bernard Henderson and C. Calvert

Many years ago, Kanaya, a maker of clogs, lived with his wife in the city of Nara. This man was known as an honest workman, and therefore had no lack of customers, so that he and his wife, Kiyu, might have lived in comfort, and very happily, but for one bitter sorrow. All their married life they had yearned for children, and had made many pilgrimages, especially to the shrines of Jizo, wearying the god with passionate prayers for a family.

But none had been granted them. And now that they were old, when work was over for the day, they would sit in silence round the warmth of the *hibachi*, not so much because the air was chill, but because of the coldness within their hearts.

One evening the clog maker, having closed the shop, sat down in the inner room to wait for his wife. She had gone out that afternoon, in spite of a heavy rain storm and, returning at dusk, had hastily left again. Kanaya was surprised and anxious at her long absence. Lately he had noticed a strangeness in Kiyu's manner; she had also been away from home during a part of every morning, and often in the afternoon as well.

He was relieved, therefore, when he heard her come in. She lingered a few moments in the shop and then, entering the room, silently began to prepare their evening meal. It seemed to Kanaya that her eyes sparkled, and that she moved with an odd, joyous lightness.

When the meal was over and the table cleared, Kiyu sat down beside Kanaya and, laying her hand on his, said, "Honourable husband, I have today done a very foolish thing for which, no doubt, our neighbours would think me mad. But you, I feel sure, will understand."

She rose eagerly, went out into the shop, and returned, bearing in her arms a large parcel wrapped in fine rice paper.

Sitting down, she laid it tenderly on her knees, removed the covering, and showed her astonished husband a boy doll of unusual size and workmanship. "This doll is called Tokutaro," said she.

It was a fantastic figure, large as a child of three years. The face was beautiful and perfectly modelled, the locks and eyelashes were of real hair, the feet and hands so carefully fashioned that they seemed those of a living child, and the clothes were of the richest flowered silk. So lifelike was the doll that the old man held his breath.

After a while he reached out timidly and felt Tokutaro's face, then the hands and feet, on which his wife pointed out the small, rosy nails, weeping for joy as she did so. Tears came into Kanaya's eyes.

"Truly," he said, "never till now have I understood 'The Sadness of Might Have Been!' But the will of the gods must be done! And now, tell me, how did you light on this rare wonder?"

Kiyu, resting her head on his shoulder, answered, "Did I not know you would understand! It may be that I am mistaken, but

I think Jizo has at last taken pity on our loneliness. This is my tale.

"A week ago, in the shop of our neighbour, Teoyo, among the vases, armour, cabinets, and other old and choice things in which he deals, I saw the doll, and my heart leaped out to it. I looked long, and then walked away with difficulty, for it seemed to me that its eyes were fixed eagerly on mine. That look haunted me day and night. I said to myself that it was a foolish fancy, born of the yearning of a childless woman, but I could not master my longing. Every day, in the morning and in the afternoon, I stood outside the shop trembling lest Tokutaro should be sold.

"On the fourth day, desperate with desire, I went in and enquired the price. Teoyo demanded twenty *ryos*, and I did not try to bargain, knowing that he is a stubborn man. Very unwillingly I went away, for I could not think of wasting so much of your hard-earned money on a whim. But, the next day I returned, and the following day also, morning and evening.

"This afternoon, as I stood outside the shop in the driving rain that had cleared the street, Teoyo suddenly called me. His voice was very gentle and strange.

" 'Neighbour,' he said, 'very surely your heart is set on this doll, for not the gods themselves could lure anyone to such faithful pilgrimages as you have made here these seven days. It is plain that some deity is concerned in this; but you shall judge. Every morning I have found Tokutaro's cheeks so stained with weeping that I have found it difficult to clear away the traces. Nor is this all. Last night Jizo appeared to me in a dream, commanding me to let you have the doll. Take it, therefore, and give me what you will, or even nothing at all, for it is not well to bargain with the gods.'

"But I, my husband, did not think it right to take advantage of his compassion, and refused the gift except at a fair price. Thereupon he told me that he had paid five *ryos* for the doll. This sum he would gladly take, but nothing more, on condition that I did not mention the matter to anyone. So I hastened home for the money, and when the business was settled, I remember how Tokutaro seemed to smile at me.

"I feel sure that the doll once belonged to some great family and was much loved. Many a little one must have fondled him, and so given him life, for I feel that in some way Tokutaro is more than wood and plaster. Have we not often heard how these figures acquire a soul if they are tenderly loved?"

"Honourable wife," Kanaya answered, "you have done wisely and well. Already it seems to me that our house is less empty. Tokutaro shall not want for love, even though it is an old and withered one. We will, however, keep this matter a secret between us. I fear the jests of our neighbours."

On the morrow they contrived a hiding place for Tokutaro, out of which, when they were alone, they would take him and feast their eyes on his beauty. Kiyu was never weary of fondling him. And when the old couple sat down to their meals, they would laughingly offer him food.

Indeed, before long they began to regard Tokutaro as a living child—their own flesh and blood. Many a time, while busy at the household work, Kiyu sang the words of a poet:

> "As flowers seem sweetest, when they pierce
>   The barren winter snow,
>   Dear Blossom of my withered age,
>   Lovely art thou, aglow
>   With beauty, like dream children seen
>   Through the slow, silent rain
>   Of tears with which I craved for thee
>   So long, my son, in vain!"

In spite of all their caution, news of these doings spread, but,

far from deriding the childless couple, neighbours spoke reverently of their seeming folly, so that after a while the old people did not hide the matter. Children took to haunting the house in order to play with Tokutaro, and the place was full of young laughter and voices, to the joy of Kanaya and his wife.

Their pleasure in the figure increased daily. When the weather was cold they would lay Tokutaro, wrapped in warm clothing, between them in the bed and fall asleep, happier for such company.

But they were to experience yet greater joys, for gradually they became aware of strange happenings.

At night it often seemed to them that a tiny hand was fondling their faces, and that a frail form was nestling close to them for warmth. Yet, when roused by the touch, nothing stirred, and wistfully, they fell asleep again. So great was their yearning that neither spoke of these experiences, but each was aware that the other knew.

One winter night Kanaya, wakened by gentle fingers that seemed unusually insistent, heard a stealthy sound.

Someone was stirring in the shop!

Before he could rise the shoji were withdrawn, and he saw two robbers enter with swords. Threatening violence, they demanded money.

Roused by their voices, Kiyu sat up and gave a cry, not of fear but of wonder, for she beheld Tokutaro standing before the men. Their eyes, glazed by terror, were fixed on the doll. The figure raised its right arm and waved away the robbers who fled in panic from the shop.

Kanaya lit the lantern and saw his wife kneeling before Tokutaro, who was lying once more on the bed. His eyes and smile were those of a living child.

There was no more sleep for the old people that night; till dawn they knelt side by side, speaking in whispers about their son.

Some weeks after, about midnight, Kiyu was awakened by light anxious fingers on her cheek. Looking up, she hastily roused her husband, for a steady roar of fire filled the air. By the shoji that closed the entrance into the shop stood Tokutaro, beckoning to them.

They snatched up a few valuables, took their little hoard of money from its hiding place, together with the image of Jizo, and

followed Tokutaro out into the street. It was empty of people, but filled with the flickering lights and shadows of fire. Flames were gushing out of their neighbour's house which, the next moment, flared like a torch. A red wave leaped out, washed over their own dwelling, and swept up towards the stars in a fountain of crimson fire.

Tokutaro led them across the road, where he stopped, leaning motionless against the wall. The old woman caught him up in her arms, while Kanaya hastened to help his neighbours who were pouring out into the red-lit street.

By this time their own house had become a roaring furnace, fed by the wooden soles of the clogs stacked in the shop. Had they delayed but a few moments, they would have perished.

Many months later, when Kanaya and his wife had rebuilt their house, they set up a special altar to Jizo, and before it, in a lacquer cabinet, Tokutaro had a place of honour; for after the fire, awe mingled with the old people's love.

Some years after, Kanaya died; and for months the forlorn wife, gazing into Tokutaro's eyes, saw them filled with tears and sorrow, answering hers.

She sold the shop and withdrew to a small country house. There she lived with Tokutaro, blessing the mercy of the gods who had so comforted her old age.

It was her delight to clothe Tokutaro in robes of costly silk. Hour upon hour she sat looking upon him, glorious as a butterfly. Moreover, unlike mortal children, his beauty was untouched by time.

One thought troubled Kiyu: what would become of her treasure after she was dead? Surely the gods, whose instrument he had been, would provide! Nevertheless, to make the future more certain, she went to the priests of the Temple of Jizo and entrusted Tokutaro to their keeping after she had gone from this world.

Two years later, neighbours found Kiyu dead, holding Tokutaro in her arms. But when the priests from the Temple of Jizo arrived to claim the wonderful doll, Tokutaro could not be found, nor was he ever again seen familiarly among men.

Mourners, however, returning home from the graveyard on the first day of the Festival of the Dead, declared they had beheld Tokutaro making offerings, burning incense, and pouring water over the tomb-stones of Kanaya and his wife.

THE TOWN IN THE LIBRARY

"Very well," said the Mouse, "then I will tell you. It is a great secret, but there is only one way to get out of this kind of town. You —I hardly know how to explain—you—you just walk out of the gate, you know."

"Dear me," said Rosamund; "I never thought of that."

Besides her children's novels, which everyone knows, E. Nesbit wrote a number of short stories for the young. The extraordinary story here should be of particular interest to Nesbit-readers because of its close links with her own life. To begin with, Rosamund and Fabian were part of her own family—they were the third and fourth of the five Bland children. (E. Nesbit was also Mrs Bland; she too comes into the tale.) More than this, the making of an imaginary town scene out of any objects around was her own invention, and was very much part of the Blands' childhood. The whole thing started when one of the little boys was trying to make an Indian fort out of building bricks and could not get the right eastern atmosphere. E. Nesbit solved the problem with some chessmen, a brass bowl and a book or two. The idea did not lie down. Out of it came her strange novel *The Magic City*, nearly a dozen years later, in 1910. Sadly, by this time, Fabian had died very suddenly at the age of fifteen. The story keeps him alive —real boy and girl, real house, real toys.

THE TOWN IN THE LIBRARY

E. Nesbit

ROSAMUND and Fabian were left alone in the library. You may
not believe this; but I advise you to believe everything I tell you,
because it is true. Truth is stranger than story-books, and when
you grow up you will hear people say this till you grow quite
sick of listening to them: you will then want to write the strangest
story that ever was—just to show that *some* stories can be stranger
than truth.

Mother was obliged to leave the children alone, because Nurse
was ill with measles, which seems a babyish thing for a grown-up
nurse to have—but it is quite true. If I had wanted to make up
anything I could have said she was ill of a broken heart or a brain-
fever, which always happens in books. But I wish to speak the
truth even if it sounds silly. And it *was* measles.

Mother could not stay with the children, because it was Christmas Eve, and on that day a lot of poor old people came up to get
their Christmas presents, tea and snuff, and flannel petticoats, and
warm capes, and boxes of needles and cottons and things like that.
Generally the children helped to give out the presents, but this
year Mother was afraid they might be going to have measles
themselves, and measles is a nasty forward illness with no manners
at all. You can catch it from a person before they know they've
got it.

So the children were left alone. Before Mother went away she said, "Look here, dears, you may play with your bricks, or make pictures with your pretty blocks that kind Uncle Thomas gave you, but you must not touch the two top-drawers of the bureau. Now don't forget. And if you're good you shall have tea with me, and perhaps there will be cake. Now you *will* be good, won't you?"

Fabian and Rosamund promised faithfully that they would be *very* good and that they would not touch the two top-drawers, and Mother went away to see about the flannel petticoats and the tea and snuff and tobacco and things.

When the children were left alone, Fabian said, "I am going to be very good. I shall be much more good than Mother expects me to."

"We *won't* look in the drawers," said Rosamund, stroking the shiny top of the bureau.

"We won't even *think* about the insides of the drawers," said Fabian. He stroked the bureau too and his fingers left four long streaks on it, because he had been eating toffee.

"I suppose," he said presently, "we may open the two *bottom* drawers? Mother couldn't have made a mistake—could she?"

So they opened the two bottom drawers just to be sure that Mother hadn't made a mistake, and to see whether there was anything in the bottom drawers that they ought not to look at.

But the bottom drawer of all had only old magazines in it. And the next to the bottom drawer had a lot of papers in it. The children knew at once by the look of the papers that they belonged to Father's great work about the Domestic Life of the Ancient Druids and they knew it was not right—or even interesting—to try to read other people's papers.

So they shut the drawers and looked at each other, and Fabian said, "I think it would be right to play with the bricks and the pretty blocks that Uncle Thomas gave us."

But Rosamund was younger than Fabian, and she said, "I am tired of the blocks, and I am tired of Uncle Thomas. I would rather look in the drawers."

"So would I," said Fabian. And they stood looking at the bureau.

Perhaps you don't know what a bureau is—children learn very little at school nowadays—so I will tell you that a bureau is a kind of chest of drawers. Sometimes it has a bookcase on the top of it, and instead of the two little top corner drawers like the chest of drawers in a bedroom it has a sloping lid, and when it is quite open you pull out two little boards underneath—and then it makes a sort of shelf for people to write letters on. The shelf lies quite flat, and lets you see little drawers inside with mother of pearl handles—and a row of pigeon holes—(which are not holes pigeons live in, but places for keeping the letters carrier-pigeons could carry round their necks if they liked). And there is very often a tiny cupboard in the middle of the bureau, with a pattern on the door in different coloured woods. So now you know.

Fabian stood first on one leg and then on the other, till Rosamund said, "Well, you might as well pull up your socks."

So he did. His socks were always just like a concertina or a very expensive photographic camera, but he used to say it was not his fault, and I suppose he knew best.

Then he said, "I say, Rom! Mother only said we weren't to *touch* the two top-drawers——"

"I *should* like to be good," said Rosamund.

"I *mean* to be good," said Fabian. "But if you took the little thin poker that is not kept for best you could put it through one of the brass handles and I could hold the other handle with the tongs. And when we could open the drawer without touching it."

"So we could! How clever you are, Fabe," said Rosamund. And she admired her brother very much. So they took the poker and the tongs. The front of the bureau got a little scratched, but the top drawer came open, and there they saw two boxes with glass tops and narrow gold paper going all round; though you could only see paper shavings through the glass they knew it was soldiers. Besides these boxes there was a doll and a donkey standing on a green grass plot that had wooden wheels, and a little wicker-work doll's cradle, and some brass cannons, and a bag that looked like marbles, and some flags, and a mouse that seemed as though it moved with clockwork; only, of course, they had promised not to touch the drawer, so they could not make sure. They looked at each other, and Fabian said:

"I wish it was tomorrow!"

You have seen that Fabian was quite a clever boy; and he knew at once that these were the Christmas presents which Santa Claus had brought for him and Rosamund. But Rosamund said, "Oh dear, I wish we hadn't!"

However, she consented to open the other drawer—without touching it, of course, because she had promised faithfully—and when, with the poker and tongs, the other drawer came open, there were large wooden boxes—the kind that hold raisins and figs—and round boxes with paper on—smooth on the top and folded in pleats round the edge; and the children knew what was inside without looking. Everyone knows what candied fruit looks like on the outside of the box. There were square boxes, too—the kind that have crackers in—with a cracker going off on the lid, very different in size and brightness from what it does really, for, as no doubt you know, a cracker very often comes in two quite calmly, without any pop at all, and then you only have the motto and the sweet, which is never nice. Of course, if there is anything else in the cracker, such as brooches or rings, you have to let the little girl who sits next to you at supper have it.

When they had pushed back the drawer Fabian said, "Let us pull out the writing drawer and make a castle."

So they pulled the drawer out and put it on the floor. Please do not try to do this if your father has a bureau, because it leads to trouble. It was only because this one was broken that they were able to do it.

Then they began to build. They had the two boxes of bricks—the wooden bricks with the pillars and the coloured glass windows, and the rational bricks which are made of clay like tiles. When all the bricks were used up they got the pretty picture blocks that kind Uncle Thomas gave them, and they built with these; but one box of blocks does not go far. Picture blocks are only good for building, except just at first. When you have made the pictures a few times you know exactly how they go, and then what's the good? This is a fault which belongs to many very expensive toys. These blocks had six pictures—Windsor Castle with the Royal Standard hoisted; ducks in a pond, with a very handsome green and blue drake; Rebecca at the well; a snowball fight—but none of the boys knew how to chuck a snowball; the Harvest Home; and the Death of Nelson.

These did not go far, as I said. There are six times as few blocks as there are pictures, because every block has six sides. If you don't understand this it shows they don't teach arithmetic at your school, or else that you don't do your home lessons.

But the best of a library is the books. Rosamund and Fabian made up with books. They got Shakespeare in fourteen volumes, and Rollin's *Ancient History* and Gibbon's *Decline and Fall*, and *The Beauties of Literature* in fifty-six fat little volumes, and they built not only a castle, but a town—and a big town—that presently towered high above them on the top of the bureau.

"It's almost big enough to get into," said Fabian, "if we had some steps." So they made steps with the *British Essayists*, the *Spectator* and the *Rambler*, and the *Observer*, and the *Tatler*; and when the steps were done they walked up them.

You may think that they could not have walked up these steps and into a town they had built themselves, but I assure you people have often done it, and anyway this is a true story. They had made a lovely gateway with two fat volumes of Macaulay and Milton's poetical works on top, and as they went through it they felt all the feelings which people have to feel when they are tourists and see really fine architecture. (Architecture means buildings, but it is a grander word, as you see.)

Rosamund and Fabian simply walked up the steps into the town they had built. Whether they got larger or the town got smaller, I do not pretend to say. When they had gone under the great gateway they found that they were in a street which they could not remember building. But they were not disagreeable about it, and they said it was a very nice street all the same.

There was a large square in the middle of the town, with seats, and there they sat down, in the town they had made, and wondered how they could have been so clever as to build it. Then they went to the walls of the town—high, strong walls built of the *Encyclopaedia* and the *Biographical Dictionary*—and far away over the brown plain of the carpet they saw a great thing like a square mountain. It was very shiny. And as they looked at it a great slice of it pushed itself out, and Fabian saw the brass handles shine, and he said:

"Why, Rom, that's the bureau."

"It's larger than I want it to be," said Rosamund, who was a little frightened. And indeed it did seem to be an extra size, for it was higher than the town.

The drawer of the great mountain bureau opened slowly, and the children could see something moving inside; then they saw the glass lid of one of the boxes go slowly up till it stood on end and looked like one side of the Crystal Palace, it was so large— and inside the box they saw something moving. The shavings and tissue-paper and the cotton-wool heaved and tossed like a sea when it is rough and you wish you had not come for a sail. And then from among the heaving whiteness came out a blue soldier, and another and another. They let themselves down from the drawer with ropes of shavings, and when they were all out there were fifty of them—foot soldiers with rifles and fixed bayonets, as well as a thin captain on a horse and a sergeant and a drummer.

The drummer beat his drum and the whole company formed

fours and marched straight for the town. They seemed to be quite full-size soldiers—indeed, *extra large*.

The children were very frightened. They left the walls and ran up and down the streets of the town trying to find a place to hide.

"Oh, there's our very own house," cried Rosamund at last; "we shall be safe there." She was surprised as well as pleased to find their own house inside the town they had built.

So they ran in, and into the library, and there was the bureau and the town they had built, and it was all small and quite the proper size. But when they looked out of the window it was not their own street, but the one they had built; they could see two volumes of the *Beauties of Literature* and the head of Rebecca in the house opposite, and down the street was the Mausoleum they had built after the pattern given in the red and yellow book that went with the bricks. It was all very confusing.

Suddenly, as they stood looking out of the windows, they heard a shouting, and there were the blue soldiers coming along the street by twos, and when the Captain got opposite their house he called out, "Fabian! Rosamund! come down!"

And they had to, for they were very much frightened.

Then the Captain said, "We have taken this town, and you are our prisoners. Do not attempt to escape, or I don't know what will happen to you."

The children explained that they had built the town, so they thought it was theirs; but the captain said very politely, "That doesn't follow at all. It's our town now. And I want provisions for my soldiers."

"We haven't any," said Fabian, but Rosamund nudged him, and said, "Won't the soldiers be very fierce if they are hungry?"

The Blue Captain heard her, and said, "You are quite right, little girl. If you have any food, produce it. It will be a generous act, and may stop any unpleasantness. My soldiers *are* very fierce. Besides," he added in a lower tone, speaking behind his hand, "you need only feed the soldiers in the usual way."

When the children heard this their minds were made up.

"If you do not mind waiting a minute," said Fabian, politely, "I will bring down any little things I can find."

Then he took his tongs, and Rosamund took the poker, and they opened the drawer where the raisins and figs and dried fruits were—for everything in the library in the town was just the same as in the library at home—and they carried them out into the big square where the Captain had drawn up his blue regiment. And here the soldiers were fed. I suppose you know how tin soldiers are fed? But children learn so little at school nowadays that I daresay you don't, so I will tell you. You just put a bit of the fig or raisin, or whatever it is, on the soldier's tin bayonet—or his sword, if he is a cavalry man—and you let it stay on till you are tired of playing at giving the soldiers rations, and then of course *you eat it for him.* This was the way in which Fabian and Rosamund fed the starving blue soldiers. But when they had done so, the soldiers were as hungry as ever.

So then the Blue Captain, who had not had anything, even on the point of his sword, said, "More—more, my gallant men are fainting for lack of food."

So there was nothing for it but to bring out the candied fruits, and to feed the soldiers with them. So Fabian and Rosamund stuck bits of candied apricot and fig and pear and cherry and beetroot on the tops of the soldiers' bayonets, and when every soldier had a piece they put a fat candied cherry on the officer's sword. Then the children knew the soldiers would be quiet for a few minutes, and they ran back into their own house and into the library to talk to each other about what they had better do, for they both felt that the blue soldiers were a very hard-hearted set of men.

"They might shut us up in the dungeons," said Rosamund, "and then Mother might lock us in, when she shut up the lid of the bureau, and we should starve to death."

"I think it's all nonsense," said Fabian. But when they looked out of the window there was the house with Windsor Castle and the head of Rebecca just opposite.

"If we could only find Mother," said Rosamund; but they knew without looking that Mother was not in the house that they were in then.

"I wish we had that mouse that looked like clockwork—and the donkey, and the other box of soldiers—perhaps they are red ones, and they would fight the blue and lick them—because red-coats are English and they always win," said Fabian.

And then Rosamund said, "Oh, Fabe, I believe we could go into *this* town, too, if we tried!"

So they went to the bureau drawer, and Rosamund got out the other box of soldiers and the mouse—it *was* a clockwork one—and the donkey with panniers, and put them in the town, while Fabian ate up a few odd raisins that had dropped on the floor.

When all the soldiers (they *were* red) were arranged on the ramparts of the little town, Fabian said, "I'm sure we can get into this town," and sure enough they did, just as they had done into the first one. And it was exactly the same sort of town as the other.

So now they were in a town built in a library in a house in a town built in a library in a house in a town called London—and the town they were in now had red soldiers in it and they felt quite safe, and the Union Jack was stuck up over the gateway. It was a stiff little flag they had found with some others in the bureau drawer; it was meant to be stuck in the Christmas pudding, but they had stuck it between two blocks and put it over the gate of their town. They walked about this town and found their own house, just as before, and went in, and there was the toy town on the floor; and you will see that they might have walked into that town also, but they saw that it was no good, and that they couldn't get out that way, but would only get deeper and deeper into a nest of towns in libraries in houses in towns in libraries in houses in towns in . . . and so on for always—something like Chinese puzzle-boxes multiplied by millions and millions for ever and ever. And they did not like even to think of this, because of course they would be getting further and further from home every time. And when Fabian explained all this to Rosamund she said he made her head ache, and she began to cry.

Then Fabian thumped her on the back and told her not to be a little silly, for he was a very kind brother. And he said, "Come out and let's see if the soldiers can tell us what to do."

So they went out; but the red soldiers said they knew nothing but drill, and even the Red Captain said he really couldn't advise. Then they met the clockwork mouse. He was big like an elephant, and the donkey with panniers was as big as a mastodon or a megatherium. (If they teach you anything at school of course they have taught you all about the megatherium and the mastodon.)

The Mouse kindly stopped to speak to the children, and Rosamund burst into tears again and said she wanted to go home.

The great Mouse looked down at her and said, "I am sorry for *you*, but your brother is the kind of child that overwinds clockwork mice the very first day he has them. I prefer to stay this size, and you to stay small."

Then Fabian said: "On my honour, I won't. If we get back

home I'll give you to Rosamund. That is, supposing I get you for one of my Christmas presents."

The donkey with panniers said, "And you won't put coals in my panniers or unglue my feet from my green grass-plot because I look more natural without wheels?"

"I give you my word," said Fabian, "I wouldn't think of such a thing."

"Very well," said the Mouse, "then I will tell you. It is a great secret, but there is only one way to get out of this kind of town. You—I hardly know how to explain—you—you just *walk out of the gate*, you know."

"Dear me," said Rosamund; "I never thought of that!"

So they all went to the gate of the town and walked out, and there they were in the library again. But when they looked out of the window the Mausoleum was still to be seen, and the terrible blue soldiers.

"What are we to do now?" asked Rosamund; but the clock-work mouse and the donkey with panniers were their proper size again now (or else the children had got bigger. It is no use asking me which, for I do not know), and so of course they could not speak.

"We must walk out of this town as we did out of the other," said Fabian.

"Yes," Rosamund said; "only this town is full of blue soldiers and I am afraid of them. Don't you think it would do if we *ran* out?"

So out they ran and down the steps that were made of the *Spectator* and the *Rambler* and the *Tatler* and the *Observer*. And directly they stood on the brown library carpet they ran to the window and looked out, and they saw—instead of the building with Windsor Castle and Rebecca's head in it—they saw their own road with the trees without any leaves and the man was just going along lighting the lamps with the stick that the gas-light pops out of, like a bird, to roost in the glass cage at the top of the lamp-post. So they knew that they were safe at home again.

And as they stood looking out they heard the library door open, and Mother's voice saying, "What a dreadful muddle! And what have you done with the raisins and the candied fruits?" And her voice was very grave indeed.

Now you will see that it was quite impossible for Fabian and

Rosamund to explain to their mother what they had done with the raisins and things, and how they had been in a town in a library in a house in a town they had built in their own library with the books and the bricks and the pretty picture blocks kind Uncle Thomas gave them. Because they were much younger than I am, and even I have found it rather hard to explain.

So Rosamund said, "Oh, Mother, my head does ache so," and began to cry. And Fabian said nothing, but he, also, began to cry.

And Mother said, "I don't wonder your head aches, after all those sweet things." And she looked as if she would like to cry too.

"I don't know what Daddy will say," said Mother, and then she gave them each a nasty powder and put them both to bed.

"I wonder what he *will* say," said Fabian just before he went to sleep.

"*I* don't know," said Rosamund, and, strange to say, they don't know to this hour what Daddy said. Because next day they both had measles, and when they got better everyone had forgotten about what had happened on Christmas Eve. And Fabian and Rosamund had forgotten just as much as everybody else. So I should never have heard of it but for the clockwork mouse. It was he who told me the story, just as the children told it to him in the town in the library in the house in the town they built in their own library with the books and the bricks and the pretty picture blocks which were given to them by kind Uncle Thomas. And if you do not believe the story it is not my fault: I believe every word the mouse said, for I know the good character of that clockwork mouse, and I know it could not tell an untruth even if it tried.

DOLLY'S ADVENTURE

Jo Donovan

DOLLY's home again
after her week's adventure
in an unknown flat.

We had some trouble
getting her from the small girl,
who meant to keep her.

Dangling by one arm
in grubby resignation
she has been returned,

and now sits dreaming
in her solitary way
upon the sofa.

But there's a new look
on her small angelic face
since last we saw her:

a look of knowledge
in the heavy-lidded eyes
that's disconcerting,

and a careless way
of wearing any garment,
that seems abandoned,

as though she had been
passed from hand to grasping hand
by many children.

Steadfastly the bear
and golliwog regard her
from the big arm-chair.

Their honest faces,
simple to stupidity,
are disapproving.

It seems quite likely
she'll be left yet more alone
after her troubles.

Poor Dolly! Her life,
lately so full and varied,
may now be irksome;
it's true that she belongs here,
but can we make her happy?

GERTRUDE'S CHILD

Gertrude walked on . . . All of a sudden she saw the old man standing at the door of a small road-side shop.

"Hullo!" she said. "Now tell me who buys your children?"

"Oh mostly dolls like yourself do," said the old man. "Or else other toys. And puppies of course, but puppies don't often have money enough—they spend it too fast. Sometimes I sell one to a pony. But ponies seldom want children very much—they're too happy playing about by themselves. As for kittens . . ."

Richard Hughes (1900–76) is best known for his novel *A High Wind in Jamaica* (1929) but he did write a number of short stories for children. Others may be found in the collections called *The Spider's Palace* and *The Wonder-Dog*. He lived for most of his life in Wales; he had a very good understanding of children as well as of dolls (there were quite a few of both around his house) and you can count on him for a truly remarkable tale.

GERTRUDE'S CHILD

Richard Hughes

ONE night, Gertrude the wooden doll got furious because the little girl she belonged to was being unkind to her.

"I won't belong to you any more!" said Gertrude: "I don't want to belong to anyone, only myself."

So Gertrude ran away. I mean, she ran *right* away—right along the main road out into the world on her own; and the night was dark.

Gertrude was glad she was made of wood and not easily hurt, for her hard little wooden feet went clickety-clop on the hard road without any shoes yet didn't get sore. She was painted with oil paint, too, so the rain just ran off her. Also, wooden dolls don't need any dinner. At dolls' parties they eat what you give them of course, and enjoy it; but in between parties wooden dolls need eat nothing at all.

Nearly Gertrude felt sorry for the little girl she had run away from, for being made of that soft stuff all children are made of which scratches and bruises so easily, and falls ill . . . But no, for Gertrude was wooden and hard right through, and *couldn't* be sorry for someone who'd been unkind to her. "I hope she falls down and bleeds!" said Gertrude to herself: "That's what she deserves!"

Then daylight came, and the sun came out and dried Gertrude, and made the paint on her hard wooden shoulders smell good. She began to sing (quite loud, though her voice was woody).

But all that day Gertrude met no one at all on the road, and began to feel lonely. She thought that it might be nice after all to have a friend—not a soft one of course, but a sensible hard one like herself. So Gertrude made up a story in her head about another wooden doll, and pretended this other wooden doll was walking beside her and talking to her (but it wasn't, of course: she was quite alone really).

When it got dark again Gertrude looked up at the face of the moon, because it was the only face round there to look at. "You're not much company, Moon!" said Gertrude. "But that's all right because I don't really *want* company." (This wasn't quite true, though she wished it was.)

But she had not walked very much farther when she came up behind an old man carrying a load on his back. The old man took her hand, and they walked along together hand-in-hand for a while. But he didn't say anything to her—not a word. "Very old men never do know what to say to dolls," Gertrude told herself.

But at last the old man stopped outside a cottage, and then he did speak to her, "Would you like a little girl of your own?" he asked Gertrude.

"No!" said Gertrude. "I don't want to belong to any little girl again, ever!"

"You don't understand," said the old man. "*You* wouldn't belong to *her*, *she* would belong to *you*."

"I don't see how . . ." said Gertrude.

"Come round to my shop in the morning and I'll explain,"
said the old man. "You see, I sell little girls in my shop. And little
boys too, if you'd rather."

"Who *on earth* wants to buy them?" asked Gertrude, astonished.

"I'll tell you tomorrow," said the old man. "Good night for
now!"

He went into his cottage and shut the door.

Gertrude walked on. She wondered who he sold little girls to.
Suppose she bought one: would a little girl turn out more trouble
than she was worth? Certainly no child could be as good company

for Gertrude as a real doll would be—but perhaps dolls couldn't buy *dolls*. . . .

Gertrude had felt very lonely while it was dark, but when morning came she did not feel quite so lonely and so she forgot the idea of buying herself a child. She was thinking of something quite different, when all of a sudden she saw the old man standing at the door of a small road-side shop.

Seeing him made her remember. "Hullo!" she said. "*Now* tell me who buys your children?"

"Oh, mostly dolls like yourself do," said the old man. "Or else other toys. And puppies of course; but puppies don't often have money enough—they spend it too fast. Sometimes I sell one to a pony. But ponies seldom want children very much—they're too happy playing about by themselves. As for kittens . . . I don't really like selling children to kittens, because kittens can be so cruel!"

"What kind of children do you sell?" asked Gertrude.

"I sell all kinds and all ages," said the old man. "Fat ones and thin ones, pretty and plain, good ones and naughty ones. You'll see some in the shop-window here, but I've lots more inside."

Gertrude looked in the window. It was got up to look like a Christmas party. Children of all sizes were sitting about in their very best clothes. Little girls had no creases at all in their pretty dresses; little boys had clean hands, and their hair was all smarmed down and oiled. The children looked stiff and shy, like people having their photographs taken. Not one of them wriggled: being

stared at in a window like this made them even too shy to pull the
crackers they held in their hands.

When she saw them, a great longing came over Gertrude to
have one of her own. "Oh, I *must* have one of those grand-looking
ones!" said Gertrude.

"Come and look at the others inside before you make up your
mind," said the old man, and led her into the shop.

Inside, Gertrude saw piles of children all over everywhere—
every kind of child you could think of: as well as English ones
there were Spanish and Russian and Dutch, and some Africans,
and a special shelf of Chinese ones, and even an Indian pair who
were brown.

There was, too, one very shining and precious child in a box by herself, who lay very still. "That's a *most* beautiful one," Gertrude whispered.

"Yes, but she wouldn't be any good to you," said the old man very sadly: "She doesn't move at all now. Her eyes won't open any more."

Still, there were plenty of children to choose from. Some were sitting in rows on the shelves (which were too high for them to climb down without help). Because it was the middle of the morning they were all eating biscuits and drinking glasses of milk.

"Can they sing?" Gertrude asked.

"Of course they can sing!" said the old man. He waved his hand, and the children stopped munching their biscuits and sang Gertrude's favourite song.

"Now that you've seen them all you'd better choose one," said the old man.

"May I feel them first?" asked Gertrude, because she couldn't believe they were real.

"Yes, if your hands are clean," said the old man.

So Gertrude poked them with her hard wooden fingers and felt their ribs, and the ones who were ticklish giggled and squealed no end. "Now you've poked them enough," said the old man. "Hurry up and choose, before you've made them all spill their milk."

Gertrude liked nearly all of them. But there was one little girl she was certain sure she would best like to have for her own. This little girl was about six-years-old, and a bit thin: she had curly yellow hair and a pretty pink dress, and short white socks, and a happy look in her eye.

"If she's naughty," thought Gertrude, "I'll smack her and smack her and smack her! That's the only way of making them good," thought Gertrude (since that was how she'd been treated herself).

But the old man seemed to know what she was thinking, and said to Gertrude, "If I sell her to you, you must promise to be kind to her! Remember, children aren't hard like you wooden dolls. If you drag *children* by the leg head-down through bushes, they get scratched and bruised. If you drop them from the top of

the stairs, they break their necks. If you take their clothes off and leave them out in the cold, they get ill. If you forget to feed them they die, just like animal pets do."

"Oh, I promise to be kind to her," said Gertrude. "But you said about her clothes—do you mean her clothes really take off?"

"Of course they do!" said the old man: "But remember what I said about being kind to her, and not letting her catch cold."

"Yes yes!" said Gertrude, even more hurriedly. Quickly she paid the price, then caught her little girl by the arm and ran out of the shop with her.

"Don't forget to give her her dinner!" the old man shouted after them.

"Good-bye! Good-bye, child!" called all the children left on the shelf (all except the very beautiful one in the box whose eyes wouldn't open).

Gertrude was delighted with her child. At first all she wanted to do was to walk up and down the street, leading her child by the hand.

Gertrude saw other dolls and puppies and people like that taking *their* children out for a walk, and she hoped they were jealous of her for having such a pretty one. But soon she got tired of this, and then she began to remember all the many things you have to do when you have a child to look after: all the washing and minding and mending for her, and feeding and cleaning and cooking and catching and combing and teaching and sewing and cuddling and bandaging and reading aloud. You couldn't do all that just wandering around: it meant having a home.

"There's a house just round the corner from here we could live in," said the child.

"And I'm going to call you Annie," said Gertrude. "You can't manage without a name."

"Good!" said the child, "I'm Annie, then," And together they went in through the gate.

Inside the gate, in front of the house there was a beautiful garden, with flowers growing. But round the back there was an orchard, so they went straight there to explore it.

Suddenly Gertrude began wondering if what the old man had said was true and Annie's clothes really did come off: for she feared that they might be sewed to her skin, the way a doll's clothes sometimes are. She took Annie's pretty pink dress off, just to find out . . . "I'll remember to put it on her again *for certain*," thought Gertrude.

Then she went on undressing Annie, dropping her clothes on the ground. "Stop undressing me, it's c-c-cold!" said Annie.

"Nonsense!" said Gertrude. "I must just find out if they *all* really unbutton."

Annie tried to run away, but Gertrude kept catching her and taking off one thing more. Annie was so hard to catch that Gertrude kept dropping the clothes all over everywhere. The sun had gone in now, and it started to snow. "Oooooo! I'm so *cold*!" shivered Annie.

"Nonsense!" said Gertrude (who never felt cold herself, of course). "You're not a bit cold really, so don't make a fuss!" And she undressed Annie completely.

When there were no more clothes to take off, Gertrude left Annie and started making snowballs to throw at the birds. Annie sat on the ground all bare, and shivered and howled. Annie couldn't find her clothes to put on again because they were all buried by now in the falling snow.

But at last Gertrude got tired of snowballing the birds. "Come on in. Don't sit there dawdling around," she said to Annie. "Come into the house!"

"Is it dinner-time yet?" asked Annie, her teeth chattering. "It feels like it must be."

"*Dinner?*" said Gertrude. "Yes—later on. But first I must cut your hair."

So Gertrude took a pair of scissors and began cutting Annie's lovely hair. But she soon found she had cut off too much on one side, which meant she then had to cut more off the other to match; and so it went on, till Annie's head had hardly any hair left. Then Gertrude was sad, because nothing was left to cut.

"Is it dinner-time *now*?" asked Annie, when her hair was all gone.

"No, you bad child! It's your bed-time," said Gertrude.

It wasn't really anywhere near bed-time, but Gertrude was cross with Annie for looking like a scarecrow with her hair all cut off. Besides, she wanted to be free of the child for a bit, to think her own thoughts. So she filled the bath with warm water, dropped Annie in as quick as she could, and then went away and left her there in the bath!

Gertrude went off to explore the house. It was a wonderful house, with cupboards everywhere—and every sort of thing you could want was there in the cupboards, all ready to hand! Gertrude spent hours and hours exploring the house, and came at last to the kitchen. There on the table was a whole pound of sausages. "I think I'll have some supper, for once," said Gertrude to herself. So she cooked the sausages, then sat down in front of the kitchen stove and ate them all up.

As she finished the last of them Gertrude felt sleepy, so went straight upstairs and got into a bed. She had forgotten all about poor Annie, left sitting there in the bath!

It was not till Gertrude was just dropping off to sleep that at last she remembered Annie. "Poor Annie!" she thought: "How horrible, having to pass the whole night in the bath!" But it was very, very dark; and Gertrude didn't want to get out of bed. "Perhaps she *likes* sleeping in baths better than beds," Gertrude told herself. "Yes I'm sure Annie would *rather* stop all night in the bath . . ."

Yet Gertrude knew in her heart that this couldn't be true. Only a fish (or a mermaid) could like sleeping in water all night. "Come on, Gertrude!" she said to herself: "Up you get!"

Gertrude jumped out of bed, and taking two torches (one for each hand) she ran to the bathroom. There was Annie, still sitting in the water, which by now was quite cold. Annie looked very sad, and her teeth were chattering. But Gertrude soon had her out of the water, and dried her with a towel, and carried Annie off with her to bed.

"Darling Annie!" said Gertrude in bed, putting her hard wooden arm round Annie's neck.

"Darling Doll!" said Annie. "How kind to me you are!"

And so they both fell asleep, with their arms tight round each other.

When they woke in the morning, Annie had a cold in her head. Her nose was red, and dripping. She had no hair, and no clothes. She didn't look pretty now, as she had in the shop.

"I must make you some new clothes, now that you've lost your others," said Gertrude. So she took the cloth off the table and cut it up and made it into clothes. But they were not very nice clothes, because Gertrude had never learned sewing. Indeed Gertrude had hardly any idea at all about how to make clothes. All the same, Annie seemed just as pleased as if her tablecloth dress was the most beautiful dress in the world.

"What are we going to do today?" asked Annie, admiring her new dress in the mirror.

"We're going to have a party," said Gertrude: "It's your birthday today! But first you have to be smacked for losing your clothes."

It wasn't fair for Annie to be smacked, because it was Gertrude herself who had lost them. But Annie just said, "I'm sorry, and I won't do it again."

" 'Sorry' is not enough! You'll have to be punished as well," said Gertrude.

Annie howled when Gertrude smacked her (and so would *you* howl if somebody smacked you with hard wooden hands!). But Gertrude didn't know how much she was hurting, of course.

"Stop crying at once, now!" said Gertrude as soon as the smacking was over. "It's time to get ready for the party."

So all the morning they made cakes and baked them, and put icing on top to look like flowers. Then they set out the candles, and hung up red paper streamers to make the room look pretty, and phoned people asking them to come.

At three in the afternoon they heard someone knock on the door. Annie wanted to open it. But Gertrude sent her up to the bathroom to wash her hands. "Wait in the bathroom till I come up to see you're really clean!" Gertrude called up the stairs after Annie, and went to open the door herself.

It was the first guest come for the party. There on the step stood a big teddy-bear, leading a very small boy by the hand.

"Come in, and be a good boy," the toy bear whispered to his little boy as Gertrude let them in. "And remember you mustn't shout for things: you must wait till the cakes are offered you, and say 'Thank you'."

"Yes, Uncle Teddy," said the little boy (but he wasn't really listening).

Next came a rocking-horse. *He* had to be helped up the steps by the three children he had brought with him. One pulled in front and two pushed behind. The children looked very proud to belong to such a fine horse.

Then came a small dumpy doll, dragging with her quite a big lanky schoolgirl. "Surely you're too old to belong to a doll!" Gertrude burst out when she saw her.

"That's what *I* think," said the big girl. "But she has had me since I was tiny, years ago—and now she won't believe I'm almost grown-up!"

"Don't talk so daft, Miss Theodora!" said the doll severely: "You're no more than a big baby still—and don't you forget it! Now, you behave nicely or I'll punish you!"

The little doll looked so fierce that the big girl was afraid of her. "S-sorry," the big girl said, and put her thumb in her mouth.

Next came a puppy, dragging a small boy behind him on a rope. The puppy marched straight in without even a 'How-d'you-do' to Gertrude and jumped up into a chair at the table where the food was spread out. The little boy tried to climb up beside him, but "Lie down!" barked the puppy to the little boy, "or you'll be tied up outside and not have any cakes at all!"

So the little boy crept under the table, and curled up by his master's chair.

Then all the dolls and toys climbed into chairs. But their children were not allowed at table at all! The children had to sit in a row on a bench in the corner: only the puppy's little boy was allowed to stay curled up on the floor, chewing his rope.

"You be good!" shouted all the dolls and toys to the children

together. "Then perhaps we'll let you have some bread-and-butter, if by the time we've finished the cakes we can't eat any more ourselves."

"I hear you have a child too, haven't you?" the teddy-bear asked Gertrude with his mouth full of chocolate biscuit. "Where is she?"

Goodness gracious! Once again Gertrude had altogether forgotten Annie after sending her up to the bathroom to wash her hands!

But Gertrude looked round the party, and saw all those proud toys with their charming fashion-magazine children, in their very best clothes, sitting so good and neat in the corner; and Gertrude felt ashamed of Annie with her tablecloth dress, and no hair, and her nose all runny. Gertrude couldn't bear all these grand toys to see Annie, or even to know she owned a child who looked so common and shabby.

Then Gertrude told a lie: "Annie's been naughty," she said. "I had to send her to bed for a punishment." (Poor Annie! And this was *her* birthday party, after all!)

"Never mind," said the teddy-bear. "It's probably just as well. If she's a naughty child I'm sure I don't want *my* little boy to meet her. She might make him naughty too."

"Quite right!" said all the other toys together. "I'm sure if she's naughty we none of us want *our* children to play with her!"

Gertrude began to feel she wasn't liking this party any longer . . .

Just then they heard a scream from the garden outside, and the puppy's little boy got up and ran to the window, trailing his rope. "I say!" he cried out, very excited. "It's a—"

"Lie down!" barked the puppy. "And don't speak till you're spoken to!"

"But it's a—"

"Do as you're told!" yapped the puppy: so the little boy became quiet.

"But I saw it too!" said one of the other children. "It was—"

"Be quiet or I'll rock on you!" said the rocking-horse, furious.

"I *won't* be quiet!" said the child bravely. "There's a lion in the garden, and he has caught Gertrude's child and is eating her up!"

"Well, well," said the teddy-bear: "What a *very* naughty little girl she must be, to need to be eaten by a lion!"

"It sounds horrid and vulgar," said the prim little doll that the big girl belonged to. "I'm sure I don't want to hear anything about it till I've finished my tea."

"Quite right!" said the teddy-bear. "It's spoiling my appetite too! Let us talk of pleasanter subjects."

"I think I would like some more ice-cream," said the rocking-horse: "If Annie is being eaten by a lion there's no use saving any for *her*."

But Gertrude sprang to her feet in a blazing rage. "You brutes and horrors and pigs!" Gertrude cried. "You're not going just to sit there and *let* her be eaten, are you?"

"It's none of *our* business," said the party.

But Gertrude didn't wait.

She seized the teapot in one hand and a spoon in the other and jumped out of the window. There was the lion, skulking about in the garden with Annie in his mouth, looking for a comfortable place to lie down and eat her.

"Drop her!" cried Gertrude. "Put my child down at once, Sir!"

But the lion only growled, and flicked his tail.

Poor Annie was very frightened, and not screaming now. The lion was huge. But Gertrude didn't wait for a moment: she threw the teapot full of hot tea right in his face and sprang at him with the spoon.

The lion roared with pain from the hot tea and dropped Annie —but instead, he seized Gertrude's arm in his teeth.

"Run, Annie!" cried Gertrude. "Run in the house and be safe!"

"I *won't* run and leave you to be eaten!" cried Annie.

Annie tore up handfuls of snow and started pelting the lion to make him let go of Gertrude's arm, but—scrunch! The lion had bitten Gertrude's arm right off.

"*Ugh!*" growled the lion, "she's only made of wood after all, and I don't like eating wooden people one bit!"

Meanwhile all the children had jumped out of the window (leaving the toys to finish the ice-cream) and were pelting and booing the lion.

"I suppose they're all made of wood too, and don't taste as nice as they look," grumbled the lion, trying with his claws to get the wood splinters out of his teeth.

Just then a big ball of snow hit the lion slap in the eye. He dropped Gertrude's arm on the ground, and ran right away, and was gone.

But Gertrude had lost her arm. "Oh, *poor* Gertrude!" said Annie.

"Never mind," said Gertrude bravely. "It doesn't hurt *too* much."

"How lucky you're made of wood and don't feel things the way we do!" said Annie.

"Y-y-yes," said Gertrude, trying her best not to cry.

But it was hard for her not to cry, for something strange was happening to Gertrude: never in all her life had she felt so *un-wooden* as now! Indeed her gone arm was hurting her horribly—almost as if she wasn't a doll, but a person.

Then the brave little boy who belonged to the rocking-horse picked up Gertrude's chewed arm and examined it. "I think I can mend this," he said, "with my carpentry tools." So he mended Gertrude's arm and fixed it on again, and the children all cheered.

Then the children went back indoors, because the toys they belonged to (and also the puppy) were calling angrily from the window. But Gertrude and Annie stopped outside together.

"Annie!" said Gertrude. "Listen. I think it's a stupid idea, dolls *having* to belong to children or children to dolls. Why can't they just be friends?"

"And both look after each other?"

"Yes. Anyway, that's how *we* are going to be from now on," said Gertrude: "You won't belong to me and I won't belong to you—not neither. So, now let us start on our travels!"

Then Annie and Gertrude put their arms round each other's waists, and started along that hard black road together. And the curious thing was this: Annie thought Gertrude's arm now felt soft, and warm—almost like the arm of another child: while Gertrude found Annie's arm comforting and *strong*—almost as if it too were a wooden one.

That's all about Gertrude and Annie for now. . . .

THE DOLL'S HOUSE

"Open it quickly, someone!"
The hook at the side was stuck fast. Pat prised it open with his
penknife, and the whole house front swung back, and—there you
were, gazing at one and the same moment into the drawing-room
and dining-room, the kitchen and two bedrooms. That is the way
for a house to open. Why don't all houses open that way?

Katherine Mansfield (1888–1923) was born and brought up in
New Zealand. Although it was later, in England, that she became
a writer, many of her short stories are set in the New Zealand that
she knew as a child. Well, the landscapes may be different, but
children, nice and nasty, poor and rich, are (like dolls and doll's
houses) much the same anywhere, as everyone who reads this
unforgettable story will agree. Kezia (who comes into other
Mansfield stories) is the author herself as a child.

THE DOLL'S HOUSE

Katherine Mansfield

W HEN dear old Mrs Hay went back to town after staying with the Burnells she sent the children a doll's house. It was so big that the carter and Pat carried it into the courtyard, and there it stayed, propped up on two wooden boxes beside the feed-room door. No harm could come to it; it was summer. And perhaps the smell of paint would have gone off by the time it had to be taken in. For, really, the smell of paint coming from that doll's house ("Sweet of old Mrs Hay, of course; most sweet and generous!")— but the smell of paint was quite enough to make anyone seriously ill, in Aunt Beryl's opinion. Even before the sacking was taken off. And when it was . . .

There stood the doll's house, a dark, oily, spinach green, picked out with bright yellow. Its two solid little chimneys, glued on to the roof, were painted red and white, and the door, gleaming with yellow varnish, was like a little slab of toffee. Four windows, real windows, were divided into panes by a broad streak of green. There was actually a tiny porch, too, painted yellow, with big lumps of congealed paint hanging along the edge.

But perfect, perfect little house! Who could possibly mind the smell. It was part of the joy, part of the newness.

"Open it quickly, someone!"

The hook at the side was stuck fast. Pat prised it open with his penknife, and the whole house front swung back, and—there you were, gazing at one and the same moment into the drawing-room and dining-room, the kitchen and two bedrooms. That is the way for a house to open! Why don't all houses open like that? How much more exciting than peering through the slit of a door into a mean little hall with a hat-stand and two umbrellas! That is—isn't it?—what you long to know about a house when you put your hand on the knocker. Perhaps it is the way God opens houses at the dead of night when He is taking a quiet turn with an angel . . .

"Oh-oh!" The Burnell children sounded as though they were in despair. It was too marvellous; it was too much for them. They had never seen anything like it in their lives. All the rooms were papered. There were pictures on the walls, painted on the paper, with gold frames complete. Red carpet covered all the floors except the kitchen; red plush chairs in the drawing-room, green in the dining-room; tables, beds with real bedclothes, a cradle, a stove, a dresser with tiny plates and one big jug. But what Kezia liked more than anything, what she liked frightfully, was the lamp. It stood in the middle of the dining-room table, an exquisite little amber lamp with a white globe. It was even filled all ready for lighting, though, of course, you couldn't light it. But there was something inside that looked like oil and moved when you shook it.

The father and mother dolls, who sprawled very stiff as though they had fainted in the drawing-room, and their two little children

asleep upstairs, were really too big for the doll's house. They didn't look as though they belonged. But the lamp was perfect. It seemed to smile at Kezia, to say, "I live here." The lamp was real.

The Burnell children could hardly walk to school fast enough the next morning. They burned to tell everybody, to describe, to—well—to boast about their doll's house before the school-bell rang.

"I'm to tell," said Isabel, "because I'm the eldest. And you two can join in after. But I'm to tell first."

There was nothing to answer. Isabel was bossy, but she was always right, and Lottie and Kezia knew too well the powers that went with being eldest. They brushed through the thick buttercups at the road edge and said nothing.

"And I'm to choose who's to come and see it first. Mother said I might."

For it had been arranged that while the doll's house stood in the courtyard they might ask the girls at school, two at a time, to come and look. Not to stay to tea, of course, or to come traipsing through the house. But just to stand quietly in the courtyard while Isabel pointed out the beauties, and Lottie and Kezia looked pleased. . . .

But hurry as they might, by the time they had reached the tarred palings of the boys' playground the bell had begun to jangle. They only just had time to whip off their hats and fall into line before the roll was called. Never mind. Isabel tried to make up for it by looking very important and mysterious and by whispering behind her hand to the girls near her, "Got something to tell you at playtime."

Playtime came and Isabel was surrounded. The girls of her class nearly fought to put their arms round her, to walk away with her, to beam flatteringly, to be her special friend. She held quite a court under the huge pine trees at the side of the play-ground. Nudging, giggling together, the little girls pressed up close. And the only two who stayed outside the ring were the two who were always outside, the little Kelveys. They knew better than to come anywhere near the Burnells.

For the fact was, the school the Burnell children went to was not at all the kind of place their parents would have chosen if there had been any choice. But there was none. It was the only school for miles. And the consequence was all the children of the neighbourhood, the Judge's little girls, the doctor's daughters, the store-keeper's children, the milkman's, were forced to mix together. Not to speak of there being an equal number of rude, rough little boys as well. But the line had to be drawn somewhere. It was drawn at the Kelveys. Many of the children, including the Burnells, were not allowed even to speak to them. They walked past the Kelveys with their heads in the air, and as they set the fashion in all matters of behaviour, the Kelveys were shunned by everybody. Even the teacher had a special voice for them, and a special smile for the other children when Lil Kelvey came up to her desk with a bunch of dreadfully common-looking flowers.

They were the daughters of a spry, hard-working little washer-woman, who went about from house to house by the day. This was awful enough. But where was Mr Kelvey? Nobody knew for certain. But everybody said he was in prison. So they were the daughters of a washerwoman and a gaolbird. Very nice company for other people's children! And they looked it. Why Mrs Kelvey made them so conspicuous was hard to understand. The truth was they were dressed in "bits" given to her by the people for whom she worked. Lil, for instance, who was a stout, plain child, with big freckles, came to school in a dress made from a green art-serge tablecloth of the Burnells', with red plush sleeves from the Logans' curtains. Her hat, perched on top of her high forehead, was a grown-up woman's hat, once the property of Miss Lecky, the postmistress. It was turned up at the back and trimmed with

a large scarlet quill. What a little guy she looked! It was impossible
not to laugh. And her little sister, our Else, wore a long white
dress rather like a nightgown, and a pair of little boy's boots. But
whatever our Else wore she would have looked strange. She was
a tiny wishbone of a child, with cropped hair and enormous
solemn eyes—a little white owl. Nobody had ever seen her
smile; she scarcely ever spoke. She went through life holding on
to Lil, with a piece of Lil's skirt screwed up in her hand. Where
Lil went, our Else followed. In the playground, on the road
going to and from school, there was Lil marching in front and
our Else holding on behind. Only when she wanted anything, or
when she was out of breath, our Else gave Lil a tug, a twitch, and
Lil stopped and turned round. The Kelveys never failed to understand each other.

Now they hovered at the edge; you couldn't stop them listening. When the little girls turned round and sneered, Lil, as usual,

gave her silly, shamefaced smile, but our Else only looked.

And Isabel's voice, so very proud, went on telling. The carpet made a great sensation, but so did the beds with real bedclothes, and the stove with an oven door.

When she finished Kezia broke in. "You've forgotten the lamp, Isabel."

"Oh yes," said Isabel, "and there's a teeny little lamp, all made of yellow glass, with a white globe that stands on the dining-room table. You couldn't tell it from a real one."

"The lamp's best of all," cried Kezia. She thought Isabel wasn't making half enough of the little lamp. But nobody paid any attention. Isabel was choosing the two who were to come back with them that afternoon and see it. She chose Emmie Cole and Lena Logan. But when the others knew they were all to have a chance, they couldn't be nice enough to Isabel. One by one they put their arms round Isabel's waist and walked her off. They had something to whisper to her, a secret. "Isabel's *my* friend."

Only the little Kelveys moved away forgotten; there was nothing more for them to hear.

Days passed, and as more children saw the doll's house, the fame of it spread. It became the one subject, the rage. The one question was, "Have you seen Burnells' doll's house? Oh, ain't it lovely!" "Haven't you seen it? Oh, I say!"

Even the dinner hour was given up to talking about it. The

little girls sat under the pines eating their thick mutton sandwiches and big slabs of johnny cake spread with butter. While
always, as near as they could get, sat the Kelveys, our Else holding
on to Lil, listening too, while they chewed their jam sandwiches
out of a newspaper soaked with large red blobs.

"Mother," said Kezia, "can't I ask the Kelveys just once?"

"Certainly not, Kezia."

"But why not?"

"Run away, Kezia; you know quite well why not."

At last everybody had seen it except them. On that day the subject
rather flagged. It was the dinner hour. The children stood together
under the pine trees, and suddenly, as they looked at the Kelveys
eating out of their paper, always by themselves, always listening,
they wanted to be horrid to them. Emmie Cole started the
whisper.

"Lil Kelvey's going to be a servant when she grows up."

"O-oh, how awful!" said Isabel Burnell, and she made eyes at
Emmie.

Emmie swallowed in a very meaning way and nodded to Isabel
as she'd seen her mother do on those occasions.

"It's true—it's true—it's true," she said.

Then Lena Logan's little eyes snapped. "Shall I ask her?" she
whispered.

"Bet you don't," said Jessie May.

"Pooh, I'm not frightened," said Lena. Suddenly she gave a
little squeal and danced in front of the other girls. "Watch!

Watch me! Watch me now!" said Lena. And sliding, gliding, dragging one foot, giggling behind her hand, Lena went over to the Kelveys.

Lil looked up from her dinner. She wrapped the rest quickly away. Our Else stopped chewing. What was coming now?

"Is it true you're going to be a servant when you grow up, Lil Kelvey?" shrilled Lena.

Dead silence. But instead of answering, Lil only gave her silly, shamefaced smile. She didn't seem to mind the question at all. What a sell for Lena! The girls began to titter.

Lena couldn't stand that. She put her hands on her hips; she shot forward. "Yah, yer father's in prison!" she hissed spitefully.

This was such a marvellous thing to have said that the little girls rushed away in a body, deeply, deeply excited, wild with joy. Someone found a long rope, and they began skipping. And never did they skip so high, run in and out so fast, or do such daring things as on that morning.

In the afternoon Pat called for the Burnell children with the buggy and they drove home. There were visitors. Isabel and Lottie, who liked visitors, went upstairs to change their pinafores. But Kezia thieved out at the back. Nobody was about; she began to swing on the big white gates of the courtyard. Presently, looking along the road, she saw two little dots. They grew bigger, they were coming towards her. Now she could see that one was in front and one close behind. Now she could see that they were the Kelveys. Kezia stopped swinging. She slipped off the gate as if she was going to run away. Then she hesitated. The Kelveys came nearer, and beside them walked their shadows, very long, stretching right across the road with their heads in the buttercups. Kezia clambered back on the gate; she had made up her mind; she swung out.

"Hullo," she said to the passing Kelveys.

They were so astounded that they stopped. Lil gave her silly smile. Our Else stared.

"You can come and see our doll's house if you want to," said Kezia, and she dragged one toe on the ground. But at that Lil turned red and shook her head quickly.

"Why not?" asked Kezia.

Lil gasped, then she said, "Your ma told our ma you wasn't to speak to us."

"Oh, well," said Kezia. She didn't know what to reply. "It doesn't matter. You can come and see our doll's house all the same. Come on. Nobody's looking."

But Lil shook her head still harder.

"Don't you want to?" asked Kezia.

Suddenly there was a twitch, a tug at Lil's skirt. She turned round. Our Else was looking at her with big, imploring eyes; she was frowning; she wanted to go. For a moment Lil looked at our Else very doubtfully. But then our Else twitched her skirt again. She started forward. Kezia led the way. Like two little stray cats they followed across the courtyard to where the doll's house stood.

"There it is," said Kezia.

There was a pause. Lil breathed loudly, almost snorted; our Else was still as stone.

"I'll open it for you," said Kezia kindly. She undid the hook and they looked inside.

"There's the drawing-room and the dining-room, and that's the—"

"Kezia!"

Oh, what a start they gave!

"Kezia!"

It was Aunt Beryl's voice. They turned round. At the back door stood Aunt Beryl, staring as if she couldn't believe what she saw.

"How dare you ask the little Kelveys into the courtyard!" said her cold, furious voice. "You know as well as I do, you're not allowed to talk to them. Run away, children, run away at once. And don't come back again," said Aunt Beryl. And she stepped into the yard and shooed them out as if they were chickens.

"Off you go immediately!" she called, cold and proud.

They did not need telling twice. Burning with shame, shrinking together, Lil huddling along like her mother, our Else dazed, somehow they crossed the big courtyard and squeezed through the white gate.

"Wicked, disobedient little girl!" said Aunt Beryl bitterly to Kezia, and she slammed the doll's house to.

The afternoon had been awful. A letter had come from Willie Brent, a terrifying, threatening letter, saying if she did not meet him that evening in Pulman's Bush, he'd come to the front door and ask the reason why! But now that she had frightened those little rats of Kelveys and given Kezia a good scolding, her heart felt lighter. That ghastly pressure was gone. She went back to the house humming.

When the Kelveys were well out of sight of Burnells', they sat down to rest on a big red drainpipe by the side of the road. Lil's cheeks were still burning; she took off the hat with the quill and held it on her knee. Dreamily they looked over the hay paddocks, past the creek, to the group of wattles where Logan's cows stood waiting to be milked. What were their thoughts?

Presently our Else nudged up close to her sister. But now she had forgotten the cross lady. She put out a finger and stroked her sister's quill; she smiled her rare smile.

"I seen the little lamp," she said softly.

Then both were silent once more.

CHINESE BALLAD

Mao Tse Tung (translated by William Empson)

Now he has seen the girl Hsiang-Hsiang:
Now back to the guerilla band.
And she goes with him down the vale.
And pauses at the strand.

The mud is yellow, broad, and thick,
And their feet stick, where the stream turns.
"Make me two models out of this,
That clutches as it yearns.

"Make one of me and one of you,
And both shall be alive
Were there no magic in the dolls
The children would not thrive.

ST. DANIEL'S CHURCH
7007 Holcomb ...ad
Box 171
Clarkston, Michigan 48016

"When you make them smash them back;
They yet can live again.
Again make dolls of you and me,
But mix them grain by grain.

"So your flesh will be part of mine,
And part of mine be yours.
Brother and sister we shall be,
Whose unity endures.

"Always the sister doll will cry,
Made in these careful ways,
Cry on and on, come back to me,
Come back, in a few days."

. . . ORMAS . . .
. . . BOOK . . .
. . . . .
. . . . . .

A DEPARTURE

"Now I've got the Noah's Ark," panted Harold, still groping wildly.

"Try to shove the lid back a bit," said Charlotte, "and pull out a dove or a zebra or a giraffe if there's one handy."

Harold toiled on with grunts and contortions, and presently produced in triumph a small grey elephant and a large beetle with a red stomach.

"They're jammed in too tight," he complained. "Can't get any more out. But as I came up, I'm sure I felt Potiphar."

A great rescue operation out of *Dream Days*. Most people today think of Kenneth Grahame (1859–1932) mainly as the author of *The Wind in the Willows*, which he wrote for his own little boy Alistair. In fact, he first made his name much earlier by two collections of stories, *The Golden Age* (1895) and *Dream Days* (1899), about a family of orphaned children, living in a country house under the unsympathetic rule of grown-up relatives ("The Olympians"). These children, Edward, Selina, Charlotte, Harold and the unnamed narrator (the second oldest), knew few others of their age, and invented their own vivid games. As you see in the story here, the toys had a rich part in their lives, even when officially passed on to the youngest of the family. All this reflects Grahame's own story, except that he was one of four orphans, not five.

A DEPARTURE

Kenneth Grahame

UNCLE Thomas was at the bottom of it. This was not the first mine he had exploded under our bows. In his favourite pursuit of fads he had passed in turn from Psychical Research to the White Rose and thence to a Children's Hospital, and we were being daily inundated with leaflets headed by a woodcut depicting Little Annie (of Poplar) sitting up in her little white cot, surrounded by the toys of the nice, kind, rich children. The idea caught on with the Olympians, always open to sentiment of a treacly, wood-cut order; and accordingly Charlotte, on entering one day dishevelled and panting, having been pursued by yelling Red-skins up to the very threshold of our peaceful home, was curtly

informed that her French lessons would begin on Monday, that she was henceforth to cease all pretence of being a trapper or a Redskin on utterly inadequate grounds, and moreover that the whole of her toys were at that moment being finally packed up in a box, for dispatch to London, to gladden the lives and bring light into the eyes of London waifs and Poplar Annies.

Naturally enough, we others received no official intimation of this grave cession of territory. We were not supposed to be interested. Harold had long ago been promoted to a knife—a recognized birthday knife. As for me, it was known that I was already given over, heart and soul, to lawless abandoned catapults —catapults which were confiscated weekly, but with which Edward kept me steadily supplied, his school having a fine tradition for excellence in their manufacture. Therefore no one was supposed to be really affected but Charlotte, and even she had already reached Miss Yonge, and should therefore have been more interested in prolific curates and harrowing deathbeds.

Notwithstanding, we all felt indignant, betrayed, and sullen to the verge of mutiny. Though for long we had affected to despise them, these toys, yet they had grown up with us, shared our joys and our sorrows, seen us at our worst, and become part of the accepted scheme of existence. As we gazed at untenanted shelves and empty, hatefully tidy corners, perhaps for the first time for long we began to do them a tardy justice.

There was old Leotard, for instance. Somehow he had come to be sadly neglected of late years—and yet how exactly he always responded to certain moods! He was an acrobat, this Leotard,

who lived in a glass-fronted box. His loose-jointed limbs were cardboard, cardboard his slender trunk; and his hands eternally grasped the bar of a trapeze. You turned the box round swiftly five or six times; the wonderful unsolved machinery worked, and Leotard swung and leapt, backwards, forwards, now astride the bar, now flying free; iron-jointed, supple-sinewed, unceasingly novel in his invention of new, unguessable attitudes; while above, below, and around him, a richly dressed audience, painted in skilful perspective of stalls, boxes, dress-circle, and gallery, watched the thrilling performance with a stolidity which seemed to mark them out as made in Germany. Hardly versatile enough perhaps, this Leotard; unsympathetic, not a companion for all hours; nor would you have chosen him to take to bed with you. And yet, within his own limits, how fresh, how engrossing, how resourceful and inventive! Well, he was gone, it seemed—merely gone. Never specially cherished while he tarried with us, he had yet contrived to build himself a particular niche of his own. Sunrise and sunset, and the dinner-bell, and the sudden rainbow, and lessons, and Leotard, and the moon through the nursery windows—they were all part of the great order of things, and the displacement of any one item seemed to disorganize the whole machinery. The immediate point was, not that the world would continue to go round as of old, but that Leotard wouldn't.

Yonder corner, now swept and garnished, had been the stall wherein the spotty horse, at the close of each laborious day, was accustomed to doze peacefully the long night through. In days of old each of us in turn had been jerked thrillingly round the room on his precarious back, had dug our heels into his unyielding sides, and had scratched our hands on the tin-tacks that secured his mane to his stiffly curving neck. Later, with increasing stature, we came to overlook his merits as a beast of burden; but how frankly, how good-naturedly, he had recognized the new conditions, and adapted himself to them without a murmur! When the military spirit was abroad, who so ready to be a squadron of cavalry, a horde of Cossacks, or artillery pounding into position? He had even served with honour as a gunboat, during a period when naval strategy was the only theme; and no false equine pride ever hindered him from taking the part of a roaring locomotive, earth-shaking, clangorous, annihilating time and space. Really it was no longer clear how life, with its manifold emergencies, was to be carried on at all without a fellow like the spotty horse, ready to step in at critical moments and take up just the part required of him.

In moments of mental depression, nothing is quite so consoling as the honest smell of a painted animal; and mechanically I turned towards the shelf that had been so long the Ararat of our weather-beaten Ark. The shelf was empty, the Ark had cast off moorings and sailed away to Poplar, and had taken with it its haunting smell, as well as that pleasant sense of disorder that the best conducted

Ark is always able to impart. The sliding roof had rarely been known to close entirely. There was always a pair of giraffe-legs sticking out, or an elephant-trunk, taking from the stiffness of its outline, and reminding us that our motley crowd of friends inside were uncomfortably cramped for room and only too ready to leap in a cascade on the floor and browse and gallop, flutter and bellow and neigh, and be their natural selves again. I think that none of us ever really thought very much of Ham and Shem and Japhet. They were only there because they were in the story, but nobody really wanted them. The Ark was built for the animals, of course—animals with tails, and trunks, and horns, and at least three legs apiece, though some unfortunates had been unable to retain even that number. And in the animals were, of course, included the birds—the dove, for instance, grey with black wings, and the red-crested woodpecker—or was it a hoopoe?—and the insects, for there was a dear beetle, about the same size as the dove, that held its own with any of the mammalia.

Of the doll-department Charlotte had naturally been sole chief for a long time; if the staff were not in their places today, it was not I who had any official right to take notice. And yet one may have been member of a Club for many a year without ever exactly understanding the use and object of the other members, until one enters, some Christmas Day or other holiday, and, surveying the deserted arm-chairs, the untenanted sofas, the barren hat-pegs, realizes, with depression, that those other fellows had their allotted functions, after all. Where was old Jerry? Where were Eugenie, Rosa, Sophy, Esmeralda? We had long drifted apart, it was true, we spoke but rarely; perhaps, absorbed in new ambitions, new achievements, I had even come to look down on these unprogressive members who were so clearly content to remain simply what they were. And now that their corners were unfilled, their chairs unoccupied—well, my eyes were opened and I wanted 'em back!

I wondered how the younger ones were taking it. The edict hit them more severely. They should have my moral countenance at any rate, if not more, in any protest or countermine they might be planning. And, indeed, something seemed possible, from the dogged, sullen air with which the two of them had trotted off in the direction of the raspberry-canes. Certain spots always had their attraction for certain moods. In love, one sought the orchard. Weary of discipline, sick of convention, impassioned for the road, the mining-camp, the land across the border, one made for the big meadow. Mutinous, sulky, charged with plots and conspiracies, one always got behind the shelter of the raspberry-canes.

"You can come too if you like," said Harold, in a subdued sort of way, as soon as he was aware that I was sitting up in bed watching him. "We didn't think you'd care, 'cos you've got two catapults. But we're goin' to do what we've settled to do, so it's no good sayin' we hadn't ought and that sort of thing, 'cos we're goin' to!"

The day had passed in an ominous peacefulness. Charlotte and Harold had kept out of my way, as well as out of everybody else's, in a purposeful manner that ought to have bred suspicion. In the

evening we had read books, or fitfully drawn ships and battles on
flyleaves, apart, in separate corners, void of conversation or
criticism, oppressed by the lowering tidiness of the universe, till
bedtime came, and disrobement, and prayers even more mechanical than usual, and lastly bed itself without so much as a giraffe
under the pillow. Harold had grunted himself between the sheets
with an ostentatious pretence of overpowering fatigue; but I
noticed that he pulled his pillow forward and propped his head
against the brass bars of his crib, and, as I was acquainted with
most of his tricks and subterfuges, it was easy for me to gather
that a painful wakefulness was his aim that night.

I had dozed off, however, and Harold was out and on his feet,
poking under the bed for his shoes, when I sat up and grimly
regarded him. Just as he said I could come if I liked, Charlotte
slipped in, her face rigid and set. And then it was borne in upon
me that I was not on in this scene. These youngsters had planned
it all out, the piece was their own, and the mounting, and the
cast. My sceptre had fallen, my rule had ceased. In this magic
hour of the summer night laws went for nothing, codes were
cancelled, and those who were most in touch with the moonlight
and the warm June spirit and the topsy-turvydom that reigns
when the clock strikes ten, were the true lords and lawmakers.

Humbly, almost timidly, I followed without a protest in the
wake of these two remorseless, purposeful young persons, who
were marching straight for the schoolroom. Here in the moonlight the grim big box stood visible—the box in which so large
a portion of our past and our personality lay entombed, cold,

swathed in paper, awaiting the carrier of the morning who would speed them forth to the strange, cold, distant Children's Hospital, where their little failings would all be misunderstood and no one would make allowances. A dreamy spectator, I stood idly by while Harold propped up the lid and the two plunged in their arms and probed and felt and grappled.

"Here's Rosa," said Harold, suddenly. "I know the feel of her hair. Will you have Rosa out?"

"Oh, give me Rosa!" cried Charlotte with a sort of gasp. And when Rosa had been dragged forth, quite unmoved apparently, placid as ever in her moon-faced contemplation of this comedy-world with its ups and downs, Charlotte retired with her to the window-seat, and there in the moonlight the two exchanged their private confidences, leaving Harold to his exploration alone.

"Here's something with sharp corners," said Harold, presently. "Must be Leotard, I think. Better let *him* go."

"Oh, yes, we can't save Leotard," assented Charlotte, limply.

Poor old Leotard! I said nothing, of course; I was not on in this piece. But, surely, had Leotard heard and rightly understood all that was going on above him, he must have sent up one feeble, strangled cry, one faint appeal to be rescued from un-familiar little Annies and retained for an audience certain to appreciate and never unduly critical.

"Now I've got to the Noah's Ark," panted Harold still groping blindly.

"Try and shove the lid back a bit," said Charlotte, "and pull out a dove or a zebra or a giraffe if there's one handy."

Harold toiled on with grunts and contortions, and presently produced in triumph a small grey elephant and a large beetle with a red stomach.

"They're jammed in too tight," he complained. "Can't get any more out. But as I came up I'm sure I felt Potiphar!" And down he dived again.

Potiphar was a finely modelled bull with a *suede* skin, rough and comfortable and warm in bed. He was my own special joy and pride, and I thrilled with honest emotion when Potiphar emerged to light once more, stout-necked and stalwart as ever.

"That'll have to do," said Charlotte, getting up. "We dursn't take any more, 'cos we'll be found out if we do. Make the box all right and bring 'em along."

Harold rammed down the wads of paper and twists of straw he had disturbed, replaced the lid squarely and innocently, and picked up his small salvage; and we sneaked off for the window most generally in use for prison-breakings and nocturnal escapades. A few seconds later and we were hurrying silently in single file along the dark edge of the lawn.

Oh, the riot, the clamour, the crowding chorus, of all silent things that spoke by scent and colour and budding thrust, that moonlit night of June! Under the laurel-shade all was still ghostly enough, brigand-haunted, crackling, whispering of night and all its possibilities of terror. But the open garden, when once we were in it—how it turned a glad new face to welcome us, glad as of old when the sunlight raked and searched it, new with the un- familiar night-aspect that yet welcomed us as guests to a hall

where the horns blew up to a new, strange banquet! Was this the same grass? could these be the same familiar flower-beds, alleys, clumps of verdure, patches of sward? At least this full white light that was flooding them was new, and accounted for all. It was Moonlight Land, and Past-Ten-o'clock Land, and we were in it and of it, and all its other denizens fully understood, and, tongue-free and awakened at last, responded and comprehended and knew. The other two, doubtless, hurrying forward full of their mission, noted little of all this. I, who was only a super, had leisure to take it all in, and, though the language and the message of the land were not all clear to me then, long afterwards I remembered and understood.

Under the farthest hedge, at the loose end of things, where the outer world began with the paddock, there was darkness once again—not the blackness that crouched so solidly under the crowding laurels, but a duskiness hung from far-spread arms of high-standing elms. There, where the small grave made a darker spot on the grey, I overtook them, only just in time to see Rosa laid stiffly out, her cherry cheeks pale in the moonlight, but her brave smile triumphant and undaunted as ever. It was a tiny grave and a shallow one, to hold so very much. Rosa once in, Potiphar, who had hitherto stood erect, stout-necked, through so many days and such various weather, must needs bow his head and lie down meekly on his side. The elephant and the beetle, equal now in a silent land where a vertebra and a red circulation counted for nothing, had to snuggle down where best they might, only a little less crowded than in their native Ark.

The earth was shovelled in and stamped down, and I was glad that no orisons were said and no speechifying took place. The whole thing was natural and right and self-explanatory, and needed no justifying or interpreting to our audience of stars and flowers. The connexion was not entirely broken now—one link remained between us and them. The Noah's Ark, with its cargo of sad-faced emigrants, might be hull down on the horizon, but two of its passengers had missed the boat and would henceforth be always near us; and, as we played above them, an elephant would understand, and a beetle would hear, and crawl again in spirit along a familiar floor. Henceforth the spotty horse would scour along far-distant plains and know the homesickness of alien stables; but Potiphar was spared maltreatment by town-bred strangers, quite capable of mistaking him for a cow. Jerry and Esmeralda might shed their limbs and their stuffing, by slow or swift degrees, in uttermost parts and unguessed corners of the globe; but Rosa's book was finally closed, and no worse fate awaited her than natural dissolution almost within touch and hail of familiar faces and objects that had been friendly to her since first she opened her eyes on a world where she had never been treated as a stranger.

As we turned to go, the man in the moon, tangled in elm-boughs, caught my eye for a moment, and I thought that never had he looked so friendly. He was going to see after them, it was evident; for he was always there, more or less, and it was no trouble to him at all, and he would tell them how things were still going, up here, and throw in a story or two of his own whenever they seemed a trifle dull. It made the going away rather easier, to know one has left somebody behind on the spot; a good fellow, too, cheery, comforting, with a fund of anecdote; a man in whom one had every confidence.

Arthur Waley (1889–1966) is best known as the great translator of Chinese and Japanese poetry and prose into English. But he did write poems of his own and this is one of them.

WHERE DO OLD THINGS GO TO?

Arthur Waley

I HAD a bicycle called "Splendid",
A cricket-bat called "The Rajah",
Eight box-kites and Scots soldiers
With kilts and red guns.
I had an album of postmarks,
A Longfellow with pictures,
Corduroy trousers that creaked,
A pencil with three colours.

Where do old things go to?
Could a cricket-bat be thrown away?
Where do the years go to?

MORE BOOKS ABOUT DOLLS

Picture Books

Ardizzone, Aingelda and Edward. THE LITTLE GIRL AND THE TINY
DOLL *Longmans* 1966
A perfect doll tale set in a modern supermarket. Doll, abandoned
in deep freeze section, hopefully waits. Nice little girl perceives,
plans rescue. 3 to 7 year olds.

Ardizzone, Aingelda and Edward. THE NIGHT RIDE *Longmans*
1973
Another inspired picture book from the same hands. Discarded
toys set off by night to find a home. 3 to 7 year olds.

Betjeman, John and Gili, Phillida. ARCHIE AND THE STRICT BAPTISTS
Murray 1978
A fine piece of Betjemania, movingly illustrated. How teddy bear
Archie, left in store-room, contrives to get to chapel after all . . .
For all age Betjemanians and teddy bear addicts.

Daly, Niki. VIM THE RAG MOUSE *Gollancz* 1979
Adventures of resilient rag mouse, removed by cat from pleasant
home, rescued by dustman, given to child, confiscated by teacher,

stolen by burglar who thereafter breaks into Vim's first home! Attractive pictures; zestful tale for 5 to 8 year olds.

Francis, Frank. NATASHA'S NEW DOLL   *Collins* 1973
Little Natasha, lost in a snowy forest, is helped to safety by wooden doll, foiling witch, finding woodcutter father. Lovely. Under-8s.

Freeman, Don. CORDUROY   *The Viking Press* 1968
Hopeful little bear waits in a toy department of a large store to be adopted and taken to a real home. 3 to 5 year olds.

Jacques, Faith. TILLY'S HOUSE   *Heinemann* 1979
Another irresistible doll picture book. Dauntless Dutch doll Tilly who feels that there must be more to life than her role of doll's house scullery maid, sets out and finds a greenhouse. What better place for a home? 4 to 7 year olds.

Jones, Harold, THERE AND BACK AGAIN   *Oxford* 1978
Enchanting little picture book, about the secret adventures of Bunby the toy rabbit, who goes out for the day in the nursery's toy sail boat, and is flown back, after a slight mishap, by a kindly pigeon. Written as well as illustrated by the artist of *The Silent Playmate*. 2 to 6 year olds.

Meyer, Renate. THE STORY OF LITTLE KNITTEL AND THREADLE *Bodley Head* 1971
An unusual doll-variant for under-8s. Little Knittel (he's knitted)

meets and marries Little Threadle (she's made of stuff). Collage pictures (see the uneven stitches) show how real they are.

Nicholson, William. CLEVER BILL   (*Heinemann* 1926) *Faber* 1979
Little girl goes on journey and forgets to pack her soldier doll, Bill Davis. But resourceful Bill (another toy soldier!) chases down the stairs, along the road, arriving at the station just in time. First published in 1926, this is a very attractive example of "Beggarstaff" style, bold, posterish, the handwritten text involved in the colourful woodcut prints. 3 to 7 year olds.

Patten, Brian and Moore, Mary. EMMA'S DOLL   *Allen & Unwin* 1976
Pale, troubled Emma, with cloudlike red hair, goes out into the night to seek help for an injured doll. Magical text and pictures. 6 to 8 year olds.

Sandburg, Carl and Pincus, Harriet. THE WEDDING PROCESSION OF THE RAG DOLL AND THE BROOM HANDLE AND WHO WAS IN IT   *Harcourt Brace Jovanovich, Inc.* 1967
A tale from Sandburg's *Rootabaga Stories* (1922) that together with the big, deliberate pictures make a strangely exciting picture book, aimed unerringly at the nursery imagination. As with Edward Lear and Andersen, things—included here Whisk Broom, Furnace Shovel, Coffee Pot—have real identity and life. 3 to 6 year olds.

Zemach, Harve and Margot. MOMMY, BUY ME A CHINA DOLL *Farrar, Straus and Giroux, Inc.* 1966
An irresistible picture book based on a splendid cumulative question-and-answer Ozark folk song. *Mommy, buy me a china doll,/Do, Mommy, do! What could we buy it with,/Eliza Lou?* Ideas soon involve the whole family as well as the farmyard. Strong, alluring pictures. 3 to 6 year olds.

Younger Stories (5 to 9 year olds)

Ainsworth, Ruth. MR JUMBLE'S TOY SHOP *Lutterworth* 1977
A full-length novel (so to speak) for readers of 5 to 9, about a delightfully friendly and most eventful toyshop.

Baker, Margaret J. HANNIBAL AND THE BEARS *Harrap* 1965
Three teddy bears, in a kindly home, are troubled about the fate of some dolls on a distant rubbish heap. With the help of Hannibal, a grave, wise, memorable elephant, they devise a rescue. See also THE SHOESHOP BEARS (1963) in which they first appear. 5 to 8 year olds.

Barrie, Margaret Stuart. MAGGIE GUMPTION 1979 MAGGIE GUMPTION FLIES HIGH 1981 *Hutchinson*
Enjoyable and perceptive tales—about dolls among dolls. Cast includes homely, reckless, "madcap" Maggie, her socialite friend Pinky Dars (kin to Lord and Lady Lardy Dars), the wooden doll Polly Flinders, who is "interesting and different" (for one thing

she wears no clothes), and the noisy, battle-mad soldiers. A treat to read. 6 to 8 year olds and up.

Bianco, Margery Williams. THE LITTLE WOODEN DOLL *Macmillan Publishing Co., Inc.* 1925
The little wooden doll in the dusty attic is found at last—but by the wrong children, who scornfully tip her over the window ledge. Never mind—her friends the mice who bring the news and the spiders who weave her a lovely dress, "like delicate lace, pure white," help her to find a good, deserving child. Another enchanting little book from top doll-writer Bianco. 5 to 8 year olds.

Goffstein, M. B. GOLDIE THE DOLLMAKER   *Farrar, Straus and Giroux, Inc.* 1969
Goldie lives near the forest where she finds the wood for making her sought-after tiny dolls, no two quite alike. "She felt responsible for the little wooden persons who could not exist but for her." Intriguing tale about the nature of "a true artist," and, for the practical, about how such toys are made. 5 to 9 year olds.

Gruelle, Johnny. RAGGEDY ANN STORIES *The Bobbs-Merrill Co.* 1918
A nursery favorite about a rag doll who is found in grandmother's attic. Full of character, ideas, and indestructible good will, she soon becomes the leader and mentor of the toys in rescues, forays, and moral decisions. "So all the other dolls were happy too, for happiness is very easy to catch when we love one another and are sweet all through." Well, she does have a candy

heart, inscribed *I Love You,* sewn inside her body. 3 to 8 year olds.

Heymans, Margriet. CATS AND DOLLS Kestrel 1975
A tiny work of genius. Little girl goes to tidy up aunt's house (aunt has sent large key in an envelope) and finds it full of mischievous cats and dolls. 8 down and others.

Hodgson Burnett, Frances. RACKETY PACKETY HOUSE *Warne* 1907
The old dolls' house in Cynthia's nursery, with its rackety lot of wooden dolls, is set aside in favour of the new Tidy Castle, with its haughty inhabitants. The irrepressible high spirits of the R.P. set remain unquenched. 8 years and above.

Jacobs, Flora Gill. THE TOY SHOP MYSTERY *Coward, McCann & Geoghegan, Inc.* 1960
Kind Mr Yodel, a cake and pastry maker, owns a rare doll house "more than 150 years old" made by skilled master-baker great-great-uncle Johann. In it—as children and Siamese cat discover—lies uncle's long-lost secret that, just in time, saves Mr Yodel's business.

Joerns, Consuelo. THE FORGOTTEN BEAR *Four Winds Press* 1978
A tiny book about a teddy bear left in attic of long unvisited summer house on deserted holiday island. One day he sends off a message in a bottle. . . . Vivid sense of the sea comes through in

the pictures—line, bear brown, and shades of sea-blue wash. 5 to 8 year olds and all bear addicts.

Jones, Harold. THE ENCHANTED NIGHT   *Faber/Transatlantic Arts* 1947
A little girl wakes on a summer night, steps into a moonlit garden, and is carried off to Toyland where broken toys are restored, and lost toys find their friends. Vintage Jones; romantic fairy-tale atmosphere caught with style in pictures and text alike. 6 to 9 years and up.

Mantle, Winifred. JONESTY IN WINTER   *Chatto & Windus* 1975
Two waifs of the toy world, Jonesty (made from an honesty pod and some grass) and Arabella (cut out of paper) wander in search of a safe winter home when frost destroys their summer abode among the nasturtiums. Movingly told; excellent detail. 3 to 8 year olds.

Milne, A. A. WINNIE-THE-POOH. THE HOUSE AT POOH CORNER *Methuen* 1926, 1928
Perhaps the best-known, most-loved toy tales in the English language, carrying with them the special sunlit, lighthearted mood of their time and setting. Note that while Pooh and the rest have human fallibility, pathos, comedy, the child remains the benevolent arbiter. All ages.

Robinson, Joan G. TEDDY ROBINSON (and many other Teddy Robinson books) *Harrap* **1953 onwards**

Gentle, lively, much-liked stories of "nice, comfortable, friendly teddy bear. He had light brown fur and kind brown eyes and he belonged to a little girl called Deborah. Wherever one of them went the other usually went too." Each tale about bedtime length. 5 to 7 year olds.

Sedgwick, Modwena. THE GALLDORA OMNIBUS *Harrap* 1973
Tales for the youngest about a home-made rag doll of so hopeful and humble a nature that every misadventure seems a lucky surprise. She has some education; she tells the scarecrow, "I know that two and two make ten, and I know the days of the week. They are yesterday, today and tomorrow." In a way, she's right. 5 to 7 year olds.

Williams, Margery. THE VELVETEEN RABBIT *Heinemann* 1922
An earlier work by the author of POOR CECCO. Shy and humble rabbit learns that when toys are truly loved, they become real. The bold, distinguished pictures by William ("Beggarstaff") Nicholson are, happily, reproduced in the latest reprint. They are of course, essential.

Williams, Ursula Moray. ADVENTURES OF THE LITTLE WOODEN HORSE *Hamish Hamilton* 1938
Our hero is the old toymaker's finest creation. But times are hard, and the old man is ill, so the wooden horse goes out to sell himself. A "quiet little horse" who doesn't really want adventure, he

gets more than his share before he at last achieves his welcome return.

Most Ages Over Nine

Bailey, Carolyn Sherwin. MISS HICKORY *Hodder & Stoughton* 1977
Though the American Newbery winner for 1947, this sterling book took 30 years to reach us here. But it's still a top doll-classic. Miss Hickory is made from an apple twig, with a hickory nut as head—thus, she has a divided temperament.

Bianco, Margery Williams. POOR CECCO *Deutsch* 1973
Perhaps the best of all the doll-novels—witty, perceptive, offering a new slant or two at every reading. For details, see Introduction. 8 years up to adults.

Clarke, Pauline. THE RETURN OF THE TWELVES *Coward, McCann & Geoghegan, Inc.* 1962
Under the attic floorboards of an old Yorkshire house, young Max finds—yes!—the Brontës' wooden soldiers. (*See* Introduction.) What's more, they move and talk. With Max's help they foil the tycoon would-be purchaser by secretly marching back to their true home in the old Brontë Parsonage—now, of course, the Museum. 8 to 10 year olds.

Godden, Rumer. THE DOLL'S HOUSE (1947); IMPUNITY JANE (1955); THE FAIRY DOLL (1956); MOUSE HOUSE (1957); THE STORY OF HOLLY

AND IVY (1958); CANDY FLOSS (1960); MISS HAPPINESS AND MISS FLOWER (1961); LITTLE PLUM (1963); HOME IS THE SAILOR (1964) and other doll tales *Macmillan*
Rumer Godden writes about dolls with the utmost sympathy and understanding—indeed, dolls are central to most of her books for the young. Her first, THE DOLL'S HOUSE, was the result of a wish to write "a novel in miniature" and this phrase applies to all these stories. Child scale and doll scale, the problems of life do not alter. Essential reading for all doll-enthusiasts. 5 to 9 year olds and others.

Greenwald, Sheila. THE SECRET IN MIRANDA'S CLOSET *Houghton Mifflin Co.* 1977
The secret is a valuable antique doll, discovered and then studied by plain child Miranda. Why the secret? Because elegant mother, who works to support them both, hated girl-toys as a child and will not impose them on her daughter. Discovery mends misunderstandings, reveals hidden talents in girl, and opens projects for both. 9 to 12 year olds.

Hoban, Russell. THE MOUSE AND HIS CHILD *Faber* 1969
One of the great fantasy landmarks of the 1960s, and one of the major doll books of our time. Clockwork mouse and child, damaged and thrown away, start on their journey, each with a different hope. "We used to dance," the mouse explains to the crow, "but now we walk. And behind us an enemy walks faster." "That's life," says the crow. Most ages.

Masefield, John. THE MIDNIGHT FOLK *Heinemann* 1927
First published in 1927, this novel remains a major children's
classic. A rich feast of fantasy—mermaids, weathercocks, a witch-
governess—but the toys who play so large a part could well go
back to the author's childhood, of which he rarely spoke. 9 years
upwards.

ACKNOWLEDGMENTS

The editor is grateful to the following authors, agents, and publishers for permission to reproduce copyrighted stories, poems, and other material in this collection:

William Heinemann Ltd. for "Rag Bag" from *Up the Airy Mountain* by Ruth Ainsworth; Heinemann Educational Ltd. for "Rag Doll" by Rachel Armstrong from *Children as Writers IV* (sponsored by W. H. Smith); Jo Donovan for "Dolly's Adventure"; J. B. Lippincott Co. for "Tokutaro" ("The Magic Child") from *Wonder Tales of Old Japan* by Bernard Henderson and C. Calvert; "Rocking-Horse Land" from *The Rat-Catcher's Daughter*, A Collection of Stories by Laurence Housman, (A Margaret K. McElderry Book), Copyright © 1974 Atheneum Publishers; Chatto & Windus for "Gertrude's Child" from *The Wonder Dog* by Richard Hughes; "The Doll's House" from *The Short Stories of Katherine Mansfield*, Copyright 1923 by Alfred A. Knopf, Inc. and renewed 1951 by J. Middleton Murry, reprinted by permission of the publisher; *Elizabeth* by Liesel Moak Skorpen, Text copyright © 1970 by Liesel Moak Skorpen, by permission of Harper & Row, Publishers, Inc.; Chatto & Windus and Mr. William Empson for "Chinese Ballad" by Mao Tse Tung from *The Collected Poems of William Empson;* Mrs. Alison Waley for "Where Do Old Things Go To?" by Arthur Waley; and "The Darkest Hour Is Just Before Dawn" from *On The Banks of Plum Creek* by Laura Ingalls Wilder, Copyright, 1937, as to text, by Harper & Row, Publishers, Inc., Renewed 1965 by Roger L. MacBride, by permission of Harper & Row, Publishers, Inc.

NIEL'S CHURCH
Holcomb Road
Box 171
kston, Michigan 48016

ST. DANIEL'S CHURCH
7007 Holcomb Road
Box 171
Clarkston, Michigan 48016

Fi
Le

Lewis, Naomi

The Silent Playmate